MW01244001

# The Safe Bet

## The Game Changer Series
## Book Three

Shealy James

The Safe Bet

Limitless Publishing, LLC
Kailua, HI 96734
www.limitlesspublishing.com

Formatting: Limitless Publishing

ISBN-13: 978-1-68058-427-1
ISBN-10: 1-68058-427-8

*"Fear is a powerful motivator. It's also the scariest."*
~Damien Rush, Class of 2015

*"Fear makes us wish for the best and hope we are brave when the bad comes."*
~Katherine Peters, Bestselling Author of Two Dimensions

*"The only thing we have to fear is fear itself."*
~Franklin D. Roosevelt

*"The only thing we have to fear is other people."*
~Reagan Anders

*"The only thing we have to fear are the demons within ourselves."*
~David Anders

*"Fear is the first step toward regret."*
~Brock Anderson

*"There's so much in the world to make me bleed."*
~Pearl Jam, "Just Breathe"

# Chapter One

My parents swore it was the happiest place on earth. It even said so on the brochure. Walking hand-in-hand in the park, I felt it. We headed straight toward the most amazing castle I had ever seen. It was the only castle I had ever seen in person, but even the ones I saw in books weren't as amazing as this one. Mickey was there, Minnie too. There were pirates and princesses and Dumbo! My mom held me tightly against her as we flew on Dumbo's back. My dad screamed wildly on a roller coaster that really wasn't scary. I was starting to believe the hype.

It was later in the day when Daddy took me on a ride without my mom. She said she was going to buy us some ice cream for when we finished the ride. I thought nothing could wipe the smile off my face. We were led by smiling workers onto a boat ride. Somehow we ended up all alone in the big boat. My dad sat behind me. "You can drive,

Reagan. Just don't hit anything."

"I don't know how to drive a boat, Daddy." He was so silly.

He laughed happily in a way that dads only laugh for their daughters. "It's a good thing the ride does it for us, then. All you have to do is sit back and relax."

I didn't want to relax. I bounced back and forth in my seat, trying to see everything. My dad was quiet as I pointed my favorite things out to him. By the end of the ride I was singing the repetitive song along with the high-pitched voices coming through the speakers.

We exited, and my dad took my hand in his to guide me to a bench. I didn't know where my mom was, but he assured me she would be there soon.

"You heard that song, right?"

I began singing it again. He shushed me, then his smile turned serious. "It's true, you know? It is a small world. Once someone enters your life, they never really leave it."

"Okay, Daddy." I went to start the song again, but he pressed a finger to my lips, quieting me once more.

"Reagan, I'm trying to tell you something important."

I frowned and looked up at his eyes. I could see now that my fearless father was sad. He even looked scared, but that couldn't be right. Dads weren't afraid of anything.

"I knew someone a long time ago, Reagan. She was the love of my life."

"No. Me and Mom are the loves of your life.

You said so."

"I do love you, but I was mistaken. Like the song says, it really is a small world, and I ran into Clara a few months ago. It was a sign, Reagan. You only cross paths with people from your past if they are really meant to be in your life. Clara was the one that got away until now. She was my high school sweetheart, my first love that I never got over. You'll understand what I mean when you're older. There are some loves from which you never recover."

"What about Mom?"

"I don't love your mom like that, and she knows it."

"I don't understand, Daddy."

"We, your mom and me, decided it's best if I don't live with you two anymore."

"Why?"

"I love Clara, so I'm going to live with her now. You need to be strong for your mom, Reagan."

"But Daddy…"

"I'm sorry, Reagan."

"But you love me!"

The look on my daddy's face was like he was looking at a big hairy spider rather than his only daughter crying in the middle of Disneyland. "Now, don't cry, Reagan. You'll make a scene."

"But you love me," I whimpered softly this time.

"It's a small world, Reagan. We'll see each other again."

My dad stood from the bench and moved to walk away. I broke down screaming. "No, Daddy!"

This time there was no mistaking the expression

on his face. He was disgusted with me. He walked away just as I felt my mom grab me from behind and hold me against her body.

Then she yelled after him, "You told her here? Today of all days? We agreed you'd wait."

He quickly turned, still walking away backwards. "I thought it'd be easier. I was wrong. Sorry."

This time when he shrugged and turned away, I screamed until tears blinded me and my throat hurt. My mom pressed my face against her and lifted my ten-year-old body from the ground. I was too big to be carried, but sometimes a girl just needed her mom to hold her. The day my father left, I needed more than the comfort from my mother to make me feel better. Ice cream and Disneyland didn't help either. It was truly the unhappiest place on earth.

# Chapter Two

## *Now*

"Reagan's doing well. She's right here," Jordan said into the phone. "You want to talk to her?" I glanced over, wondering who he could possibly be speaking to that would want anything to do with me. Even though we had lived together for over a decade, we led pretty separate lives. I had my awesome people that actually took advantage of sunlight, and he had his gamer friends who preferred Mineclash or whatever the dumb game was called to the outdoors.

"Oh? She grew tomatoes, huh?"

Ah. It was our father—well his father, my sperm donor. I hadn't bothered with my father in years while Jordan still called him weekly. I wasn't sure why Jordan bothered to ask if he wanted to speak to me since we stopped acknowledging each other years ago. If I were to guess, Dad of the Year quickly changed the subject when Jordan mentioned my name.

I rolled my eyes when Jordan added another absent comment about his mother's ridiculous new gardening endeavor. Every time a vegetable appears, his mother and our shared giver of DNA felt it was worthy of a celebration. If only he had felt that excited about his daughter…

Instead of sticking around to hear more about the glorious tomatoes, I headed to my room to change, then snuck out to our garage gym to punch the bag until I had once again forgotten my father existed and the euphoria from my good day had returned.

My father fell firmly in the category of the fool-me-thrice men. They were the ones who I let disappoint me waaaay too many times. These were the relationships that went beyond "shame on me." They were more along the lines of, "Reagan, you're a fucking moron if you let these rat bastards within five hundred feet of you ever again."

As I stood in front of the bag, I let years of disappointment wash over me.

*Jab.*

The first birthday he forgot.

*Cross.*

My high school graduation.

*Kick.*

My mother crying every time she hung up the phone after trying yet again to reach out to him.

*Jab.*

Son.

*Cross.*

Of.

*Kick.*

A.

*Kick. Kick. Kick.*

Nutcracker!

I kept up the pace until my workout was fueled by an intrinsic motivation to kick ass rather than a hate for the Let-Down King. Simply thinking of my father put a dark cloud over me until I released some serious endorphins. I shouldn't have needed this kind of workout today of all days. The cute guy that owned the restaurant on the edge of the pier added a wink to his wave as he walked by my store this morning. I was cleaning my huge bay window just in time to see him strip his wetsuit in the parking lot after his morning surf, as was our routine. I never missed a showing of Restaurant Guy's strip tease, and he never failed to give me his signature grin at the end of it. We never spoke, though. I checked him out every morning, then he'd wave, and we would go about our days until he stood at his bar and watched me lock up after a shift. I usually shot a flirty smile his way as I left. I couldn't just ignore the poor sap. It would be rude, and the flirting from afar was fun. It was exciting, and no one's heart was in any way involved, just how I liked it.

My friend Melanie had been trying to convince me to talk to Restaurant Guy for a while now. I wouldn't allow myself to ruin the game. I was happy in my quiet little world, and I didn't need someone to come along and mess up the balance I had spent years creating. I did text her about the wink just to let her think I was making progress. She replied asking if she could tell me his name yet, to which I gave her a firm no. If I knew his name then we would be one step closer to meeting, and everyone knew it was all downhill from there.

All my good feelings from Restaurant Guy's wink faded the second Jordan mentioned those tomatoes. I knew I'd be sore and bruised tomorrow after my workout, but this was why I started kickboxing in the first place—to relieve pent-up frustration. Endorphins, people. It was the way to go.

Jordan lowered the blaring Eminem song to a more reasonable decibel when he stepped into the garage.

"So, New Guy thinks I'm weird," Jordan announced, ignoring the elephant in the room. I wasn't surprised. Not only did we never talk about our father after Jordan supposedly repaired his relationship with him, but I had also been hearing about New Guy for weeks. He started at Jordan's company a month or so ago and was deemed the nickname befitting the newest guy at his work. I couldn't tell you his name, but I could tell you he was good at his job of improving and marketing the app Jordan's company created. He also surfed and climbed in his free time. Jordan was suddenly considering taking up rock climbing. The image of my gamer brother climbing rocks gave me the giggles every time I thought of it. Don't get me wrong. Jordan was in decent shape for an indoorsy guy, but his hands were soft, you know?

Usually Jordan did his very limited face-to-face socialization with his girlfriend, Zoe. At the beginning I couldn't even believe he landed a girl as great as Zoe, but somehow he had managed to get her attention and keep it over the past few years. Otherwise, his online gamer friends that were likely twelve-year-olds acted as his connection to the world. Then one day, out of nowhere, he went out for beers with New Guy and came back with a bromance of epic proportions. I had a feeling it wouldn't be long before New Guy would be gracing the rest of us with his presence.

"Did you hear me?"

"You are weird," I confirmed simply while unwrapping my hands. Eh, not too bad. Just red. No blood.

He rolled his eyes at my immaturity. I ignored him like usual and threw on the t-shirt I had draped over the chair by the door. I couldn't work out in loose clothes. It was an accident waiting to happen. I was an accident waiting to happen.

Once I was sufficiently unwrapped and covered, I headed back into the house for some after-workout treats, still pretending Jordan wasn't following me. He didn't speak again until I was sitting on the couch drinking soda and eating cheese puffs. He uncharacteristically overlooked the fact that my feet were on the furniture, and I was all sweaty. He had a one-track mind, but I was sure the reminder to keep our immaculate furniture clean would follow as soon as he was finished beating this dead horse.

"Don't you want to know why?" he continued. My brother could be really annoying.

"Because you gel your hair like it's 1998?" Way to go, Reagan. That helped bring the maturity level of this situation up to at least high school level.

"No, and my hair is fine."

9

"Because you still say the word 'rad' like it's a normal word?" Now, I just couldn't stop.

"Uh. I don't say 'rad.'"

"Because you secretly listen to Disney music when no one's around?"

"I don't do that either."

"Sure you don't," I said, shoving another processed piece of cheesy deliciousness in my mouth. "Oh! I know. Is it because—"

"Reagan! I asked if you wanted to know. I didn't say to guess."

"Yes, but I have a feeling there's a point to this that involves me getting made fun of, so I was getting my punches in first. I'm a winner, Jordan."

"That's the dumbest thing you've ever said."

"Make your point, dear brother."

"Ah, yes, my point. Thanks for allowing me to get back to this, Peter Pan. New Guy—"

"Peter Pan?" I interrupted, still not allowing him to spit out what he wanted to say.

I could see the frustration lines appearing on his face. That big nasty vein was starting to poke out, and his cheeks were red. "Because you never grow up."

"Ha. I see. That's clever for you, Jordo."

"Reagan!"

Battle won. Time to move on.

"Sorry. Proceed."

"Ugh," he groaned. "New Guy thinks it's weird for me to live with my sister."

"Are you telling me you want me to move out?" I sat up straight, letting my jaw drop. A loud belch escaped me without permission right at that

10

moment, but I didn't care. Jordan had seen worse when I gave up pretenses years ago. I had dismissed good manners and dating on the same day.

"You are so pleasant to live with," he pointed out.

"Yeah? And?"

"Well, it might be time for you to consider moving into your own space."

"Seriously?"

"I mean, take your time, but yeah. You know I've been thinking about proposing. Don't think that you won't still see Meyer every day. You know you will, but I just happen to think it's time for us to move on with our lives."

"You're joking," I said, still dumbfounded by the bomb my stupid-ass brother dropped, and not only because I was worried about seeing my niece, Meyer, whenever I wanted.

"No, I'm not. And in the meantime, I told New Guy to come over for dinner."

"What? Why?"

"He's coming tonight. Meyer is at a sleepover, so it works out perfectly."

"I'll say it again, why?"

"Because he's a cool guy and new in town. He's more likely to stick around if he has friends."

"And we're going to be those friends?" I asked skeptically.

"Yes. Can you please try to be somewhat presentable? Maybe wear something a little cleaner or you know, wash your hair."

"My hair is clean, jerk!" Well, it was clean until I took out twenty years of frustration on a punching bag, which was now a complete waste of time considering my brother was kicking me out. All that stress I felt earlier was creeping back up my spine. Distraction, that's what I needed. I looked down at my old black t-shirt that used to belong to he-whose-name-I-still-can't-say-without-wanting-to cry. It was a little sweaty and now had cheesy fingerprints on it. It was time to give up on the junk food and maybe take a long shower…so long I used up all the hot water, so that my jerk brother would have to take a cold shower before his dumb friend arrived.

Jordan decided to grill out, and I did my best June Cleaver impersonation by wearing a cute floral dress and baking a pie. I seriously baked a pie. It wasn't hard. All I had to do was take it out of the box and stick it in the oven. Zoe was witness to the whole thing. I figured what the hell. If Jordan was going to kick me out, he at least needed to see the awesomeness that he'd be missing.

I had just closed the oven door when the doorbell rang. I heard male voices by the door, but Zoe and I stayed put in the kitchen, where we were sharing a bottle of wine. I may have helped make dinner, but greeting New Guy at the door was a one-person job.

Laughter rang through the house, and the sounds of both male voices were so familiar that all my hair stood at attention. My spine automatically straightened, and my stomach clenched, making me reconsider the cheese puffs from earlier. My body was clearly aware of what was to come before my mind had time to catch up. By the time my mind decided to do its job and function, the flight instinct was present in all its glory, but for some reason my body wouldn't move. Sometimes in stressful situations my brain and body refused to work in tandem.

He was in the room. I could feel him, but I couldn't turn around to let my eyes confirm what my body felt from the second that laugh rang through the house. Zoe jumped off her stool to meet her boyfriend's new friend like the good, uninformed girlfriend that she was. Completely unaware of my turmoil, she smiled and greeted him warmly, and I was grateful for her distraction. She was giving me a moment to compose myself. I needed ten more years to actually accomplish the task, but that wasn't in the cards for me right then.

"Reagan!" Jordan shouted. He was always doing that.

"What?" I snapped, turning quickly but still managing to avoid eye contact with the stranger who wasn't a stranger at all. No, instead the other man in the fool-me-thrice brigade stood in front of me. Nausea consumed me, but aside from the whole shaking like a leaf thing, I still remained frozen while my mind fought my body. My heart pounded wildly against my ribs. I should be able to stand in the same room with him after all this time, but should was a funny concept.

I should be able to see him and speak to him, but my mind went haywire every time he was near. I should be over what happened in the past. Time should heal all wounds, but it only made me fear this moment more considering I never stopped feeling so strongly for him. I had hoped it was the memory of him that had me feeling so much, but judging from the way my body responded to his presence, I knew it wasn't. He was the only man in the world who could affect me like this after a ten-year absence, and for that I hated myself a little.

"Did you hear me, Reagan?" Hear you? Can't you see I'm freaking out over here? "This is Brock Anderson, but I think you already knew that." Jordan's grin told me he was well aware who this guy was to me. A flick of my eyes to Brock told me he had made the connection as well. My guess was that the only one who was unaware that Jordan and Brock had just set me up was Zoe, but she was quickly figuring it out while we all stood there letting the tension build.

Brock grinned wickedly as he crossed the kitchen to where I stood. I feared if he came closer, I would shatter, but that didn't stop him. Nor did it finally set my body in motion. "Nice to see you again, Rea," he drawled in that gravelly bedroom voice just before he gently pressed his lips to my cheek. Before pulling away, he whispered, "I missed you."

"You two know each other?" Zoe asked, completely confused by Brock's behavior. We had been calling him New Guy all month. I would have never even considered he could have been Brock. Sure, Jordan mentioned New Guy surfs, but a lot of people surf around here. Yeah, he may have said he was from Seattle, but we were from a suburb of Seattle. It wasn't technically in the city. I didn't pay attention to what college Jordan said New Guy attended, but—ugh! Why hadn't I paid better attention?

Brock answered for me. "We go way back, don't we, Rea?"

I was still unresponsive, but no one except Zoe was concerned. Jordan's grin finally started to subside when he saw that my reaction hadn't changed. "Reagan and Brock went to school together," he explained on an awkward cough as if that was enough. It wasn't. Our story ran far deeper than two people simply attending the same school. It was the kind of story that didn't have a happy ending, so why the hell would Jordan bring this kind of trouble into our home?

I turned a nasty glare on my brother that he understood, judging by the way he threw his hands up in surrender. Jordan had just become the newest addition to the men who had fooled me thrice.

# Chapter Three

## *June 2001*

We weren't friends from the start. We were enemies first. He strolled into our class as the new kid without a care in the world, and my daddy had just left us. I hated him for his easygoing attitude. I hated him even more when the teacher made him sit next to me. I didn't feel different when he smiled at me, and I punched him in the nose the first time he offered me the chocolate cupcake his mom packed him for lunch. I took the cupcake and left him and his watering eyes at the lunch table. I kind of wanted to punch myself for turning back to have one last look at him, but it made me even angrier when he caught me looking and offered me a kind smile. All of it was so wrong.

At some point you spend enough time with someone you hate, and suddenly you don't hate the person anymore. After the hate dissipated toward the end of middle school, we became friends. We probably should have always been friends

16

considering we hung out with the same group and our moms worked together. It was like something changed that year, and it wasn't only due to the hormones. We were different, and from that point on we were ingrained in each other's lives. The next four years were a blur of happy memories that all included Brock.

"You ready to take on the world, Rea?" Brock whispered from behind me as soon as we lined up to walk into the stupid ceremony. "You look really sexy in that gown."

"Shut your face, Brock. This is the best day of your miserable existence." I heard him laugh, and I had to hide my smile so he couldn't see it.

"Nah. Yesterday afternoon was pretty great. Too bad we didn't get to finish round two."

"Shh!"

Brock moved to my school when we were in fifth grade. We were in the same class every year, but things were about to change. We were heading to college, and our bubble was about to get a whole lot bigger. I wasn't sure how I felt about that, but for now he was right beside me like he had been for the previous eight years. When your last names are Anders and Anderson, sitting next to each other was unavoidable. There were no names in between ours, at least not where we were from. It didn't help our birthdays were a day apart, we lived one street apart, both of our parents were divorced, and our moms worked together at our elementary school. We were stuck with each other, but somehow, over time, we learned to like it. Well, we more than liked it now.

17

He was back in my ear a moment later. "You riding with me to Ivy's party and finishing what we started? Your mom is letting you spend the night, right?"

"You want to do that at a party?" I spoke over my shoulder as discreetly as I could. We were in line for our high school graduation ceremony. Who knew which gossip hound was listening in? People had been trying to figure us out since we walked into high school together. It was old news, but that didn't mean they were any less interested in the latest Brock and Reagan saga. News flash! We weren't together like that. Never had been. Probably never would be.

"Why not? Everybody thinks we're together anyway. Let's give 'em something to talk about before we ditch this place."

"Probably because you're always whispering in my ear at inappropriate times. You know our moms will still be here, right? Do you want them to know everything?"

"We've been sneaking around for two years, Rea. If your mom was going to send you to that convent you're so afraid of, you'd already be gone. Now, tonight? It's on."

Yes, we were talking about what you think we were talking about. Brock and I were going to "do it" that night. We were going to go all the way, dance naked, bump uglies, whatever you want to call it. I could go on and on with the euphemisms, but surely you get the point. We were planning to have sex. When you're a teenager and live with your nosey mother, you have to plan it.

Spontaneous passion doesn't exist when your mom would lock you up for, gasp, behaving like a teenager.

"Fine, but you're my ride to the party, and I get to choose the music."

He snickered and stood back in his place before Mrs. Waverly saw he was messing up her perfect line. She had always hated the two of us. We had her for English every year. After the first time we disagreed over comparing the prejudices seen in Huck Finn to those in To Kill a Mockingbird, Brock and I decided tormenting the crazy woman was necessary. She gave me a B on my paper, but I showed her when the school's literary journal published it with the support of the principal. Brock and I spent high school disagreeing with everything Mrs. Waverly said, and I honestly think I learned more from arguing with her than anyone did listening to any other teacher.

"Deal," Brock agreed, then stepped back in line.

We still had to be careful. For one thing, I didn't want people to think we were together. Wait. No. That wasn't exactly true. I didn't want to start thinking we were together. By this point in my life I was sure I had fallen completely in love with Brock Anderson. Me, Reagan Anders, the girl who perfected playing it cool, fell for the boy who used to steal my lunch and threw up all over my math test in sixth grade. I wasn't this kind of girl. High school love was lame and only led to broken hearts. It makes me sad to think about all the high school sweethearts that marry each other and never go anywhere or do anything exciting. They are each other's excitement until suddenly one of them realizes how much they missed out on life and cheats with some trashy skank. Stupid.

That didn't mean I didn't want to experiment like every other teenager. I had a lot of attention from boys. I knew I wasn't ugly, but I was sure the morons at my school wanted to conquer the standoffish girl that hung out with all the popular kids. It wasn't going to happen.

I wasn't looking for conversation or a husband. I was on the hunt for a good time without having to worry about the whole school knowing what color the drapes were. Or was it the curtains? I couldn't ever remember.

Here's the real problem, though. If you experiment with a bunch of guys, you're a slut. If you have a boyfriend, it was socially acceptable to do the deed, but then feelings get involved. If I knew anything about life, I knew, without a doubt, gossip was a currency and feelings were messy. So, what was the solution? Secretly hook up with your best friend. It sounded good at the time. It felt even better, but it was starting to get complicated thanks to those pesky emotions.

Brock and I never acted like anything more was going on when anyone else was around. It was the only way to prevent rumors running rampant among our peers. We were only friends, best friends, as far as anyone else was concerned. That's all I thought we were myself until the day my bestie, Ivy, asked me if I liked Brock as more than a fuck buddy. It was like the sky fell. Disappointment took over my brain. I hated that I had done what every other mindless cliché at my school did: I fell for the guy. What was even worse was that I had also been caught.

I ignored Brock for the next week and a half, which was next to impossible when you sit next to each other in almost every class, but I needed to get my emotions in check. Finally he got the hint and left me alone. When I thought I could handle my newly discovered "feelings" for the rat bastard, I started talking to him again. His response? "Oh good, your period's over. I thought this one would last forever." I punched him in the stomach and walked away. It was another month before we spoke again, and I only started talking to him after he brought me a tray of chocolate cupcakes with white icing and watched Clueless and 10 Things I Hate about You with me. The cupcakes would have been enough, but he deserved some movie time for talking about my period, which I described in explicit detail in between movies. After that, he learned to leave Aunt Flo out of any and all future conversations.

Tonight was going to be more exploration for us. I acted like he was the one who wanted it so badly, but the truth was that I could hardly sit still in anticipation. Of course this made the already long and mind-numbing graduation ceremony unending and miserable. After the third speech about paving our own path or something like that, Brock talked me into paper, rock, scissors, which he called rock, paper, scissors just to annoy me. We were subtle, but we were also in the front row. When I caught Mrs. Waverly eyeing us, I grinned and pointed her out to Brock. He gave Mrs. Waverly a double thumbs-up. I swear I saw smoke come out of her ears when her face turned bright red. You couldn't have stopped my and Brock's laughter if you tried.

"How's your tattoo holding up?" he asked during the valedictorian's speech, making a point of not listening to the smug asshole standing at the podium. Topher Hayes asked me out once during junior year. I had looked at him like he was crazy. Before I could gently reject him, Brock was wrapping an arm around me and telling Topher to run along. Topher looked Brock up and down, then said, "She's out of your league." I simply rolled my eyes and walked away before they pulled out rulers to measure their dicks. Topher was cute but he wasn't a core shaker or even remotely interesting. Brock outshined him every day of the week. Fortunately, Topher wasn't too torn up when I finally rejected him. He started dating Elizabeth Short a week later, and they had been together ever since. She's following him to college next year. High school sweethearts. Blech!

I finally responded to the question as Topher started in on the "what's next" part of his speech. "Fine. It doesn't itch anymore. Yours?"

"Awesome. Am I going to get to see yours tonight?" Our birthday presents to each other this year were tattoos. No, they didn't match. He had a Celtic trinity symbol on the inside of his arm. I chose a simple watercolor feather. Our friend, Adam, once told us that feathers represented honor and respect. I liked the idea that something so delicate could mean something so powerful. I had the feather tattooed down where my bikini covered to keep it hidden from my mother, who was vehemently anti-ink.

"Are you asking if we can keep the lights on? You can come right out and say it, you know," I joked while avoiding the question.

"Maybe we should go with lights off. Then I can picture that blonde chick from that girly movie where they dance on the bar you made me watch last week."

"If you aren't careful, you'll be looking for another friend with benefits tonight."

He leaned closer to my ear. "Is that all we are?" I ignored him. Then he added, "I thought for sure you liked the benefits."

I bit my cheek to keep from smiling. "It seems I forgot. Must not have been that good."

"Whatever, Rea. Keep your legs still, then." I wanted to wipe that smug look off his face, but punching him would only give him more ammunition.

"Shut up. You have no effect on me."

"Wanna bet?"

"You're anything but a safe bet, Brock."

"Exactly." He grinned proudly, while I spent the rest of graduation wondering if it was a compliment or an insult. I was leaning toward insult when I said it, but he obviously didn't take it that way.

Finally we threw our caps in the air, and Brock lifted me from the ground in a big hug celebrating our new freedom. It was a picture perfect moment, him holding me in the air with that smile on his face. He looked happy and free, and my heart leapt.

If only I could have bottled that moment…

# Chapter Four

### *Now*

I could smell the setup. It reeked of betrayal, and there was only one way I handled the men in my life disappointing me—with a splash of drama and a whole lot of shutting down. After realizing the whole "meet the new guy" was planned, it took a few moments to regain my faculties. Once I was fully present, it was time to make my exit. I took my glorious pie off the counter and looked at my brother with the harshest glare my eyes could muster. "Go. To. Hell," I bit out quietly enough so only he could hear while Zoe and Brock continued to chat about how we knew each other. Then I took my awesome pie and headed out the door.

It should be mentioned that I lived in my own little world. Here on cloud nine, I spent my days blissfully unaware of the chaos around me. It might make me sound like an irresponsible adult, but I didn't watch the news. I paid no attention to global issues or politics. What was even better was that I let few people visit my cloud, and with three exceptions, no one was a permanent fixture there. No one new could gray my cloud. Never again would I let anyone stay past his welcome. My world was a happy place full of sunshine, rainbows, and pie...lots of pie. So, when someone came along and disrupted my lovely little existence, I did what any smart storm victim would do: I packed my shit and moved my cloud somewhere else.

My dinner, ahem—apple pie, sat in the passenger seat as I drove down to the boardwalk. I had no problem sleeping in my store with a delicious meal to keep me company. At least there would be no one there who screwed me over. I could spend my days with my imaginary friends with fictional problems and conflicts that never made me feel like I could explode at any moment. Avoidance was the game, and I was the champion.

Yes, I was well aware that storming out of my brother's house made me a drama queen. I was also aware that running away would not solve anything, nor would it make Brock go away. Jordan had been trying to convince me to see Brock for years. He did the same thing with my father. He felt I needed closure. Ha! Closure. What BS. I shot a middle finger up at "closure" and kept driving.

The store smelled of books like an old library. Since it was a used bookstore, some of the books were really old. I couldn't pass up an original copy of anything and kept them in glass cases on display. I set up the requisite "Best Seller" section along with "Indie Favorites" and "Books Everyone Should Read At Least Once" in the front. There was a huge children's books section with toys and pint size chairs. Then there was an even bigger romance section toward the back. It was my favorite, and the women around here had a lot to donate to the romance department...possibly because there was so little romance to actually keep us busy. My situation was by choice, but I was certain that wasn't the case for all the women in town.

I locked the door and quickly made my way past the bodice rippers to the loft, where there was a reading spot I made for Meyer and myself. Yeah, I was an awesome aunt, but even more than that—it was where I spent my free time away from home...the home I was about to lose. Right...

I let out a huge sigh and glanced around. The loft space was small, but there was a comfy couch up there. This wouldn't be the first time I had slept on it. Sometimes I just fell asleep reading and never went home. I remembered the days when Jordan worried, but then he realized it would likely continue to happen and let it go. Now he wanted me gone and had brought home the one person who made me want to disappear. Maybe he did it to ensure I left. I was guessing it was that damn closure thing again, though.

I kicked off my shoes and snuggled onto the couch with my favorite throw, my pie, and a fork. Once I had my book pulled up on my e-reader, I dug into my pie. I know. I know. What was a girl who owned a used bookstore doing reading on an e-reader? It was like this: they don't sell all books in paperbacks these days. There were some great e-books out there, and that was why I also sold gift cards and hosted a book club. My business would undoubtedly go under within the next five years, but that would be okay with me. I didn't like to do one thing for too long anyway. I was enjoying it while it lasted, just like my pie.

It was already halfway gone when my stomach started to revolt, but did that stop me from taking two more bites? Oh no.

My phone rang just as I considered giving up. If it was Jordan, he could shove it, but I had a sneaking suspicion it was my mother calling to check in. She was the kind of mom who only called once a week but panicked if I didn't answer the phone the one time she did, so I forced myself from the comfy couch and followed the sound of bells to my purse, which had mysteriously hidden itself under a table. I made it just in time to answer before it went to voicemail, but my mother wasn't the one on the other end.

"Reagan," a small voice cried when I answered the phone.

It took me a second to process what she said. "Meyer?" She was at a sleepover. She shouldn't be calling. To be fair, she didn't really want to go. It was only her second one, so Jordan and I were still unsure how to handle her staying overnight with friends. We encouraged it but still went over nine million rules before she left. It was our job to make sure she felt beyond loved.

"Reagan! Come get me," she wailed.

"Meyer? What's wrong?" She was crying, which had never happened before. When she was a baby, she cried maybe three times. All three times were because of poopy diapers that exploded out of her diaper like a bomb had gone off. I would have cried too if that happened to me.

"Are you coming?"

Her tone had me shooting into action. "Yes! I'm at the store, so I'll be there in like ten minutes or so."

"Hurry!"

"You want to tell me why you're upset?" I asked her as I set my pie to the side and dug in my purse for my keys.

"No. Just hurry!" she wailed then hung up on me. I glanced down at my phone in disbelief. My calm, cool niece was suddenly turning into a dramatic preteen. This was not okay. If she was becoming anything like me, we were doomed.

I rushed out of the store, almost forgetting to lock up and actually forgetting my shoes, but who cared? It was the beach and Meyer needed me. When I turned around from locking the door, I didn't look up fast enough and ran right into a brick wall.

Nope. That was definitely not a brick wall. It had clothes and…oh dear God. It was a man. My fingers were crawling up a man's chest. There were definitely feet in my field of vision.

I followed the well-defined calves up to the khaki shorts and the fitted, light blue polo to the face I had been trying to avoid. I saw my hands on his chest like an out of body experience and momentarily told myself to remember the way it felt because it had been a long time since I had my hands on a man with muscles like this. When my

29

brain and body connected after yet another malfunction, I ripped them away from him like he was a hot potato.

"I don't know what you're doing here, but I have to go," I said.

"Reagan, we have to talk."

"The time to talk was ten years ago, Brock." I stepped around him and headed toward the parking lot, only to find he had fallen in step with me.

"You aren't wearing shoes."

"I'm in a hurry." I picked up the pace to prove my point.

"Why'd you leave?"

I dashed down the stairs and prayed there weren't little pebbles, enemies of the bare feet, in the parking lot. "Because like I told you the last two times I saw you this decade, I don't want to see you." It was the simplest explanation even if it wasn't entirely true.

"Yeah, we need to talk about that." Was he seriously still following me?

There were only a few cars in the parking lot. Teens often came here to hook up on the beach only to get chased off by the cops. I was always fascinated by the people thought the sandy shore was romantic. Who wanted that shit up their crack? Even if you brought a blanket, sand still found a way of getting everywhere.

I opened my car door but it slammed and stayed closed from the big paw and meaty arm holding it shut. "Reagan! Stop running."

I hauled my body to a stop and turned to face the hulk who was currently slowing me down. "I have somewhere to be right now. Can we do this later?" And by later, I meant never.

"No. We're doing this now," he growled. That was hot, and my body responded like the repressed cavewoman she was. I shamed her and mentally reminded her to have some class.

"I can't," I ground out. "Come back tomorrow." Then, using all the strength I had left after my workout that day, I pushed the wall of muscle away. Amazingly, he let me climb in my car and drive away. My relief was short lived, though. A big truck pulled out of the parking lot behind me and followed me down the suburban streets where Meyer's friend lived. He wasn't giving up.

Pulling up to the house where I had dropped Meyer off for parties before, I climbed out of my car, hoping Brock was smart enough to stay put. He was, although he looked rather suspicious sitting in his big truck outside a ten-year-old girl's birthday party. It wasn't my problem. I wasn't the creeper in the truck.

Julie's mom was opening the front door as I climbed the steps. "Thank goodness you're here. I can't get her to come out of the bathroom."

I entered their upscale brick home like a woman on a mission. I was going to save the kid from herself and eliminate this perplexing situation from tonight's list of dramatic events. Julie's mom guided me to a bathroom on the main floor, where she knocked and alerted Meyer to my presence.

Meyer cracked the door, allowing me to see her tear-stained face as she sat on the floor of the bathroom. My heart broke a little as I took in my sweet niece hiding peeking out with swollen eyes and red cheeks. With a nod of her head, she granted me permission to enter her safe space. I dropped my purse and quickly lowered myself to her level and hugged her to me.

"What's up, kiddo?"

"I'm dying," she sobbed.

"What?" Surely I had misheard her.

"I'm bleeding from down there and the internet says I could have cancer." He sobs shook her whole body. For such a smart girl, she was really missing the boat on this one.

"Wait. Let me get this straight. You are bleeding from down there, and you looked it up online?" She nodded against me. "And the website said you have cancer." She nodded again. "It didn't say that you could be starting your period?"

"I'm too young," she cried into my shirt.

"Sorry to break it to you, but you're definitely not too young to ride the crimson wave. Welcome to womanhood, monster. It sucks."

"What about the cancer?"

"I feel confident that you don't have the cancer, but I could take you to a doctor to have your downtown checked out."

"No!" She sat up like a rocket launching and gave me a cartoonish bug-eyed look.

"All right. All right," I surrendered. "How about we handle this the way my mom did with me? Ice cream and a midnight tampon run?"

"You want me to stick something up in there?" Meyer looked horrified, which was progress from the tears and the bug-eyed, shocked look.

"No, but I find the words 'pad' and 'feminine napkin' revolting."

"I find this whole conversation revolting," she replied.

"I can't say I disagree, kid. Now let's blow this joint before my butt flattens from sitting on this pristine marble."

"What about the girls out there?"

"What about them? We'll tell them you're sick. They don't need to know anything else."

"But my pants…"

"Ah. Yes. Here." I took off the cardigan I had over my sleeveless dress. It was long on her, so it covered what it needed to hide and made her feel comfortable enough to walk out. I left her with the contents of my purse and a couple of instructions for how to deal with the merchandise. Then I headed out to find Julie's mom and Meyer's overnight bag.

Once all that was taken care of, we headed to where I parked, where Brock was still sitting waiting on me to return. I had forgotten about him during the bloody crisis. Ugh. Had I remembered, I would have probably prevented him from seeing . Meyer. He was going to ruin my ice cream run. I just knew it.

I pulled away and started to drive to the twenty-four hour grocery, but thought twice and turned to go home.

"Reagan, is that truck following us?" Meyer asked from the passenger seat as she watched the lights behind us in the side mirror.

"Yes."

"Care to explain?" Meyer was beyond her years in most things except internet searches. She spoke like an adult because we waited too long to socialize her with other kids, or so her teachers have said. Whoops.

"No."

She hummed as she glanced in the mirror, suspicious of our follower.

A red light stopped us and gave me a second to think. "How about I drop you at home with Zoe and you get a movie set up and throw on your fleece pajamas? I'll go get ice cream and essentials, then we'll stay up all night watching movies and force your dad to make us pancakes in the morning."

"Did you already tell Zoe?"

"I texted from the mega mansion we just left."

"Cool. Then I'm down. As long as I don't have to say it out loud to anyone."

I laughed. "Don't worry, monster. I've got your back."

I dropped her off, making sure she made it in the house okay and praying the big bad wolf in the truck behind me stayed put long enough for me not to have to kick his ass. Meyer gave one last curious look as she closed the front door. Thankfully, I had texted Zoe a warning, so she knew Meyer would be home. She would distract her right away from her troubles and my stalker. Not only had Zoe agreed to start movie time, but she also promised to rid the estrogen-filled family room of Jordan and his testosterone. Hopefully he understood, but Jordan wasn't known for being the most perceptive one in the house.

The door to the house had hardly shut before the door to my car flew open. My foot didn't even have a chance to transition from break to gas.

"Who was that?" Brock growled.

I turned to look him in the eye with the angriest glare I could muster for someone who was a foot away from the man who held her heart ten years ago and had yet to meet someone who could even slightly compare. He once made me the happiest girl in the world but that was then. I hated that the excitement I felt around him had never dissipated. After I had spent the last decade avoiding intense feelings, the flock of butterflies in my stomach was altogether unpleasant when mixed with the fear and hurt that time was supposed to cure.

"Get out of my car." I sounded a lot stronger than I felt.

"It's a nice car...like a tank. What does your mom think of it?"

I drove a black Hummer. It was awesome, but my mom was of the opinion that it was silly to buy such an environmentally unfriendly car. "She thinks I'm solely responsible for global warming."

"You could run someone over in that thing."

"Not when I drive like a grandma."

"Since when?" he snorted. That joke would never be funny.

"You done?" I asked, ignoring his comment about how I used to drive. He hadn't ridden with me in a long time...since before...

"Who is she, Rea?"

I didn't respond to what sounded like an accusation. Instead, I just waited for him to exit the vehicle.

"You're not going to answer? Okay. Here's what I know. She looks just like you. She's probably a little older than we were when we met, which coincidentally is about the same amount of time since you disappeared. Seeing her is like déjà vu. So tell me, Rea, is she the reason you stayed away for so long?"

Of course he thought the worst. He really believed Meyer was a secret I kept all this time. Hurt tore through me, but I gave him the truth in words laced with spite. "Yes," I choked out the lie, then gained control of my voice. "She's the reason I stayed away. Now, get the fuck out of my car."

Silence stretched between us for what seemed like minutes, but the clock didn't move while I watched the bluish or maybe greenish numbers light up the car. What was that color? Was it considered blue or green?

"I'm not leaving until you talk to me, so you might as well drive to wherever you were headed," Brock said as he buckled his seatbelt.

My body was strung tight, and I felt like I was going to explode at any second. Why, why, why wouldn't he just leave me alone?

Still parked in my spot, I white-knuckled the steering wheel. "She's not yours, if that's what you're thinking."

"That's not what I was thinking. She's just…it's like you were cloned."

"She's Jordan's daughter. That's Meyer. I'm sure he's told you about her. Now, will you leave me alone now?" I hated how I suddenly sounded weak. Only he had this kind of power over me.

"We don't have to be enemies. Just tell me what I did to make you never want to see me again, because for the life of me I can't figure it out."

When I didn't answer, he let out a frustrated sigh. Yeah? I know the feeling. I was frustrated with myself as well. I had been for a long time, and I didn't see any relief in my future.

"I can't forget about you, Reagan. If I could, I would have already." Then he climbed out of my car. Seconds later his truck roared past me, and I was left feeling like I had lost him all over again. Maybe I lost a piece of myself this time. I couldn't be sure, but I knew something was definitely broken inside of me.

Later that night, long after I had locked myself away from Brock and Jordan and the drama, the memories returned. I knew it was only a matter of time before the nightmares took over.

# Chapter Five

## *September 2008*

I saw him on a Saturday. He was just like I remembered. Maybe he had a few more tattoos, but otherwise he looked exactly the same. He approached me with his signature smirk firmly in place and a walk that spoke of his confidence. "Well, well, well, if it isn't little Reagan Anders."

"Adam!" I quickly closed the last of the distance between us and gave him a hug, forgetting for a moment that anyone from high school was an unwelcome sight. Adam was the kind of guy who made you forget your troubles. He was just Adam. He had always been different, the nice guy, the one who put everyone else before him.

"What are you doing here?"

"I'm visiting my mom. Seattle is in between us, so it's easier to meet here for a short visit. What about you?" I didn't want to tell him more on the off chance he would speak to others, one person in particular. I was still in the avoiding stage, and by avoiding Brock, I had to avoid everything else associated with him.

"I have a bar close to Pike's Place called Hank's. I just inherited it and plan to renovate it as soon as I can. Come by and have a drink sometime."

The news that he ran a bar had me pausing my escape. "What happened to painting?"

He shrugged. "It doesn't always pay the bills. There's a mural at the bar." Adam lifted a hand to scratch his jaw then added, "You should really come by, Rea."

Rea. He called me the nickname Brock used to call me. There's no way Adam could know what happened. He wasn't there. Sure, he and Brock were friends at one time and might still be, but Brock was never one to hold deep conversations with anyone...well, anyone but me.

I shook my head, trying to escape the memories. This was what I had been trying to evade. Even after all these years, thinking about Brock still pierced my heart in the most unpleasant way. It seemed it didn't matter how much time passed, the mere mention of his name caused a physical reaction so automatic that no amount of self-help books or psychology classes could make it stop. The churning sensation I was feeling paired with a dry mouth that made it difficult to swallow was only the beginning. I had been through all the defense mechanisms: denial, repression, regression, displacement, projection, reaction formation, intellectualization, rationalization, and now sublimation. I had been moving on with life. Now, it seemed Adam was forcing me to head right back into denial with one conversation.

"Reagan?" Adam said my name again with a worried expression that made me feel guilty for ignoring someone who was once a really good friend.

"Yeah, I'll stop by." I didn't know why I agreed. There had always been something about Adam. I was never attracted to him, but he had a way of suckering me in. The boy gave good woo.

"That's all I ask." Adam wrapped me in his arms. The hug was oddly comforting, considering I hadn't been really hugged by a man in…too long. No need to put a time on that in particular, but that hug was the reason I showed up at the bar. That and the promise. I make an effort to keep my promises. Being let down too many times by someone who doesn't keep his word will do that to you.

A crowded bar had never been my idea of a good time. Too many drunkards made me nervous, but tonight my anxiety stemmed from more than just the possibility of an out-of-control crowd. In the back of my mind, I kept thinking that immersing myself in Adam's world came at a huge risk.

I stepped through the door and found a sea of people already there even though it wasn't that late. The bar was dingy, like he mentioned. I could immediately see why he wanted to renovate the place. Instead of continuing to stand around and take in the poorly kept building, I headed straight to the bar and ordered a beer. The bartender was wild and obnoxious looking, and I immediately liked her style. I never had the guts to dye my hair or wear revealing clothes like she did. Her confidence was apparent, making me immediately respect her and maybe even envy her a bit.

She slid my beer across the scratched wood surface and moved on to the next customer without batting an eye. I sipped delicately, still taking in everything when my name was shouted over the roar of the music.

"Reagan!" I turned to find Adam smiling and making his way through the crowd toward me. "You came." He greeted with a hug.

"I told you I would."

"I figured you were only saying that to get away from me."

Hmm…perceptive man, aren't you, Adam?

"Honestly, I considered it," I admitted. "Cool place."

"It will be, but it's nice of you to say that. We are going to re-do all the woodwork and build a stage over there. I want to change the lighting and make it less biker bar and more upscale to pull in a younger crowd."

"We?" I foolishly asked.

"Yeah, um…" He looked over my shoulder, so I turned and came face to face with my past, the very one I had been trying to avoid since he broke my heart. He was smiling down at a beautiful blonde and then he kissed her in a way that was not really appropriate for public consumption. Of course he had a girl. He always had someone. My foolish heart jumped up in my throat. How could it still hurt to see him with someone else?

I wished I could say I was surprised to see that he was with a girl, but why would I be? Blondes were his type. The only consolation was that when he turned our way, he looked just as surprised to see me, judging by the dumbfounded expression on his face. I was sure mine matched his as I worked to school it into a bored one instead. My muscles refused to cooperate at first because my whole body had gone into some kind of shock. I feared my face was giving away my fear and discomfort, so I quickly turned back to Adam.

"Maybe you should go say hi," he said with a sympathetic tone. Clearly he knew more than he had originally let on. This had been a setup.

I was considering punching Adam in the stomach just to let out some of the boiling emotion, but I refrained. Instead of acting on impulse, training told me to turn the other direction. I ended up marching right out of the bar and was heading up the sidewalk to where my car was parked when he called my name.

"Reagan." I kept walking, knowing exactly whose voice that was. "Reagan, stop!"

My body halted its movement, and no matter how many times I told them to go, my legs refused. I heard him approach until he was standing directly behind me. Every nerve in me felt his presence. I couldn't believe the electricity was still between us. It was the same as before but maybe stronger since I hadn't experienced anything like it since the last time he held me.

"What are you doing here?" His voice was brusque and filled with anger. He was working to control it like I would if I spoke.

"Damn it, Reagan. Speak!"

White-hot rage tore through me when he treated me like I was a dog. This I could control. I swallowed the fire down into the pits of my belly and hid it with a calm façade.

I didn't know what I was going to say. It wasn't like I planned it. My pride was the last thing I had to myself, though, so when I turned and faced him, I didn't crack under the pressure of seeing his gorgeous face marred by anger that was clearly directed toward me. His eyes bored into me, looking for answers. His jaw was tight and neck was flexed. Everything about him was on the offensive. Well, join the club, buddy!

"When I was eight years old," I began, "my parents took me to Disneyland. It was right before school started, days before I met you." I paused to catch my breath, wondering why I thought of this moment to tell Brock what I needed to say. "We rode this little boat ride. It plays this annoying song over and over. That's where he told me he was leaving us. He said he loved me and wanted me, but he said the world was small and people who were meant to be in our lives would show up again."

Brock looked as confused as I felt. He remained silent but nodded, prompting me to go on.

"I thought I understood then what he meant, what the silly song was telling us, but no. It wasn't until this moment that I had some real clarity. It really is a small world. I hoped I could escape you, but I should have known that there would be no end to the torture. Maybe you're meant to be in my life, but until today I held out hope that this would never happen."

I turned and continued toward my car, but his hand grabbed my arm before I could get too far. My lungs refused to fill with air, and my heart pounded wildly. How he could cause such a reaction from me was beyond comprehension. No man had ever made me feel anything but bored. Brock could have me on my knees with one look, and I never understood it. How, after so long, could he still make me feel so much?

"Stop, Reagan. You can't just walk away."

"Watch me," I gritted out, and I tried to free my arm from his iron grip.

"No. You had your say. It's my turn."

Before he could say another word, I stepped closer to him and looked him dead in the eye. In a low voice, I said, "Let. Me. Go." His eyes flicked between mine once, then twice, before his hand loosened on my arm. Before he could say another word, I turned on my heel and ran as quickly as I could to my car. Once I was there and enclosed in the safety of its cocoon, I let myself break, but I didn't cry. There were no tears that night. Instead, I allowed myself to succumb to the lack of sensation that would keep me protected.

# Chapter Six

## *June 2001*

I wanted to scratch my eyeballs out to somehow make myself unsee what I just witnessed. A lobotomy would have been nice. Alcohol wasn't working, and I wasn't about to do anything stronger even if it was readily available at all of Ivy's parties. No matter how much I wanted an escape, that wasn't it for me.

The hour after the graduation ceremony had been a chaos of pictures and hugs before we were finally allowed to leave. I dragged Brock to his truck to show him my surprise. Right before I climbed into my seat through the door he was holding open, I unzipped my hideous graduation gown and revealed my dress. It was white, fitted, and more revealing than my mom would have liked if she had been paying attention. Brock was certainly paying attention to it, though. His eyes were wide as he looked my body top to bottom. "Damn," he groaned.

Mission accomplished. I turned up the volume on the radio as Brock drove too fast to Ivy's house jamming out to Outkast's "Ms. Jackson." He pulled around back where he parked when he was told his mom he was spending the night at Neal's." No one was there yet, and we were in our spot, hidden in the trees. Having a rich friend with a large house and even bigger yard had come in handy over the years. It also helped that her dad was in international business and never showed his face at his own million-dollar estate.

Brock unbuckled my seatbelt and pulled me astride his lap, forcing my dress to rise and uncover what little of my legs had been hidden beneath it. "I'm going to screw you in this dress," he breathed while he dragged his lips across my collarbone. We had mutually discovered that the right touches to my clavicle were…insane. Brock used those kisses as a weapon now, and I caved like every damn time. You would too if the hottest guy at your school knew your spot.

I moaned quietly, trying to escape the things he made me feel. I both loved and hated the way he could command my body with a few well-placed kisses or gentle touches. It was everything I could do not to let him see the control he had over me. "I might let you." I ground against his erection.

"Might?"

Lights filled the driveway, and we knew our friend—no, Brock's friend—Neal would be pulling his truck up next to Brock's. Playtime was over. Equal amounts of disappointment and relief flooded my body. I wanted Brock. My body was desperate for him, but my heart was ruining everything.

"Come on, you two!" Neal pounded on the hood of the truck. I hated that guy. "Ivy said her parents bought her a bottle of Dom to apologize for not showing up again." But I loved champagne.

"Ooh! Champagne." I clapped and bounced on his lap until Brock's hands latched onto my hips, effectively stopping me from unintentionally riding him.

Brock growled when I crawled off of him and out of his truck. "I can't believe I'm getting blue balls so you can drink champagne."

"It's Dom! Last time they sent some other crap. A few hours won't hurt you."

"Speak for yourself," he mumbled as he adjusted himself in his slacks. Seeing him as affected as I was gave me a thrill. I felt powerful and beautiful with Brock. He didn't use my body like most teenage boys would; he worshipped it. The fact that he sought pleasure from giving me bliss was more along the lines of a book or a movie than reality. Of course two years of experimenting and testing out scenes from smutty romance novels made our hormone-driven encounters slightly more erotic than the average teenage rendezvous and sometimes hilarious. In the end, we knew every inch of each other's bodies.

Just as I began to reconsider the rushing to the party, Ivy stepped out of the house and sang, "Reagan!" in a melodic, high-pitched voice.

Damn.

The party was a typical for graduation, drinking, dancing, and hooking up followed by puking and passing out. It should have been a good time, but it wasn't, at least not for me. Candace Wood from our rival high school showed up. Everyone knew she had a thing for Brock. She spent the whole night hanging on him. The closer he let her get, the further I remained. Jealousy wasn't a good look on anybody.

Instead I spent the whole night hanging out with another guy from our school, Adam. He was cute in a scrawny artist kind of way, but he wasn't my type. Brock was everything to me, but I couldn't let him know that. I wasn't the kind of girl who showed her cards. My poker face was unbeatable, and at the time, I thought that was a good thing. Unfortunately, Candace didn't mind showing him her hand or anything else for that matter. She was hanging on my everything like her life depended on it. And what was worse, he seemed to like it. Before the end of the night, he was taking her into a bedroom with a backwards glance as if he was checking to make sure I saw what he was doing. The smile on his face as the door closed sealed the deal for me. That was the moment I first discovered I still hated Brock like I did when I first met him. He still had that easygoing way that made everyone fall at his feet, everyone but me.

Instead of indulging further, I called my mom to come get me. She believed me when I told her I felt sick, probably because I did. She took my home and stayed with me while I threw up the contents of my stomach. She didn't once scold me for underage drinking and gave me a warm cloth for my puffy eyes and ginger ale. Yes, I was crying. I never cried.

I hated criers. I was the tough girl, the one that could beat up most of the boys. I think I scared my mom that night with all the tears. The girl who usually punched a bag to rid herself of emotions was on the bathroom floor sobbing. Not a pretty picture.

The next morning, voices coming from down the hall woke me from a dead sleep. We lived in a single-story house, so there was zero privacy except in the basement, which was terrifying in its own way.

I clearly heard the rumble of Brock speaking quietly from the direction of the kitchen, followed by my mom saying, "She's sick. She hasn't felt this bad since that time you both ended up with the stomach flu."

"I'm gonna go check on her," he announced, giving me the warning I needed. I flew out of my bed and ran into the bathroom across the hall before he could turn the corner. With the shower on, I could pretend I didn't hear him. I washed my hair in the hottest water I could stand, then let it beat over me, hoping it would burn some of the stupid out of me. Loving Brock was something I already regretted and something I unfortunately couldn't control.

I wrapped a towel in my hair and slid on my short purple robe. When I walked into my room, I was surprised to see Brock sitting against my headboard with his feet propped on my bed.

"What are you doing?"

"Waiting for you," he said as he openly eyed my body.

Ignoring the buzz that coursed through me, I pulled on yoga pants under my robe and closed the top, so no cleavage was hanging out. "And?"

Once I was covered, his eyes finally met mine. "What happened to you last night?"

"I didn't feel well, so I came home. Did you have fun?" Act like it didn't matter. I couldn't make direct eye contact or I would quite possibly turn into one of those foolish girls that begged for attention. As much as I wanted to yell at him and ask him how he could screw that awful girl, especially when I was right there, I couldn't. I refused to let him know how much he hurt me.

Through the corner of my eye I caught him looking at me with suspicion written all over his face. When I gave him nothing, he snapped out of it and said, "Yeah. It was fine."

"That's good." Hello, awkward tension that only appeared when each of us had more to say than we actually allow out of our mouths.

And Ten—Nine—Eight—Seven—

"Ready for our road trip?" There it was. He was showing me he could play this game as well as I could. Whoever made the first move was the loser. As much as I'd enjoy the consequences, I would not let him win this battle. No orgasm was worth my pride.

"Yeah. I just need to finish packing. When are Neal and Ivy meeting us?"

"In an hour. Your mom ran to the store to get us a few snacks to take with us. She didn't think you should go since you're 'sick'."

"I'm fine. She'll get over it."

He shrugged. "I hope she gets some barbecue chips this time."

"Fat chance. Get ready for apples, almonds, and organic veggie sticks." We had been on a low carb, all organic diet since my dad left when I was ten. I hid sugar from my mom the way most kids hid alcohol or drugs. Candy was my drug of choice.

"Whatever. She loves me. She'll get chips and Oreos." He smiled happily. I turned my back to him to look away from his flawless face. It was easy to be his friend, but when he smiled like that, my heart almost hurt.

"Keep dreaming, buddy," I choked out, hoping it sounded somewhat indifferent.

Our road trip was our first official act of freedom. Ivy's parents sent her a car to take because they had seen it was the best one for a road trip on some website. They didn't show up for graduation, but they bought her an unnecessary vehicle, a diamond bracelet, and let's not forget the expensive champagne. It was nice to have all these things, but I had a sneaking suspicion that Ivy would have rather grown up with my overbearing mom than new wheels every year and a thousand dollars for every good grade.

After finishing packing and hugging my mom goodbye sixteen thousand times, we were on our way. Our two-week road trip had officially begun. The first night we camped at Cape Perpetua. As soon as the boys had the tents set up, Brock shouted, "I'm not sharing a tent with Neal." It was meant to be a joke, as if anyone ever questioned the sleeping arrangements, but I kinda wished he would share a tent with Neal. I wouldn't be tempted to cuddle with Ivy or do unspeakable things to her in the middle of the night. Even more importantly, my heart wouldn't ever be on the line.

I kept my big mouth shut, though. My self-respect was on the line. No one knew I was having these horrendous feelings, and I could keep my legs closed for two weeks. I wasn't a slut for Pete's sakes. So, that was that. I was stuck sharing a tent, then a bed with Brock.

Every day there was some moment I thought he was going to give in. The first night we woke up spooning. I could feel how badly he wanted me, but you know what he did? He rolled over and faced the other way.

Another night, it was cold...really cold. He had the bright idea of combining our sleeping bags and sharing body heat, which I took as a possible invitation for more. I agreed coolly, as if it was no big deal. And then it wasn't. He really meant we were going to share body heat and nothing more.

I thought we had a breakthrough moment toward the end of the trip when we were snuggled in our tent. We had been silent for a while, and I assumed he was asleep. I couldn't close my eyes for the third night in a row. I silently begged him to give in. I might have even prayed for it, wished on a shooting star for it, and wished on a penny that I tossed into a fountain that day, but so far—nothing. Then he said, "What happened, Rea?" And I really believed this was our chance to change everything.

"What do you mean?"

Then he ruined it all by saying, "When did we

grow up and stop being kids?"

The conversation was more philosophical than honest. It was romantically a huge disappointment, but in terms of our friendship, it was exactly what I needed to connect with him again. We talked like we used to, about nothing and everything. We laughed like we always had, and the sexual tension was palpable, but nothing would have convinced me to give up that time with him. Those conversations with Brock were what made me believe that I could never live without him.

But there was still something in the back of my mind that left me wondering if he felt it as well. I needed to him to confirm it, to give me a clear indication of how he felt because as much as I hated to admit it, I wanted Brock as more than a friend or a fuck buddy. I wanted him to be mine, and I wanted to be his in every way possible. Even if we were too young, even if we were doomed to fail, I wanted it all with him.

"Brock," I started. He turned to me and looked me right in the eye. "Can I ask you something?"

"You can ask me anything, Rea. You know that." He was sincere, and it was time that I put my big girl panties on and say what needed to be said.

Just as I opened my mouth to ask about Candace, two girly screams tore from the tent next to us. Brock quickly unzipped our tent as Neal and Ivy scrambled out of theirs. "Snake!" one of them yelled. I couldn't figure out who was shouting because it was dark, and they both seemed so have freakishly high-pitched voices right then.

Once they were safely free from their now-collapsed tent, Ivy turned to us breathing heavily. "There's a snake."

"Yeah, we got that," Brock responded dryly as he grabbed a flashlight and headed to deal with the offending creature. I stayed safely hidden until I heard Neal clear his throat and say a manly, "Thank you," to his buddy, who did not scream like a two-year-old in the presence of a snake.

By the time everything calmed down, the moment was ruined, and we went to sleep without further conversation. We did, however, laugh at Neal until we were both too tired to stay awake any longer.

\*\*\*

The last day on the road arrived too quickly, as it tended to do when I was having fun. We were all exhausted and a little depressed about going home to summer jobs. Brock was going to work for his dad at his office. Neal was working construction, and I was working at a local pharmacy as a cashier while Ivy perfected her tan and read all the classics she hadn't yet had time to read (yeah, right). She should have been happy compared to the rest of us, but she was just as down about going back home as us worker bees.

The car was quiet, too quiet. It was the complete opposite of the drive out of town. On the way, Ivy and I chatted away and sang to the loud music. I was busy avoiding Brock's watchful eye and focused on having fun then. Now, I was spread out across the backseat while he held my feet in his lap and rubbed my calves. Ivy and Neal kept flipping through the radio, having an annoying silent music battle that made me wonder what crawled up their rears. A dark cloud was lingering over us as we traveled back home.

We stopped for gas about two hours away, and Ivy and I found ourselves alone while the boys ran into the station for drinks. "What if we never went back?" she asked, staring out the passenger side window where her feet were resting.

"What do you mean? Live like nomads? Skip college?"

"I don't know. Just never go home."

"My mom would love that," I said sarcastically, forgetting for a moment about her family situation.

She seemed unfazed and responded quickly. "You'd be with Brock, though."

"Yay." I groaned and fell back against the seat.

"Still nothing?" she asked.

I continued to file my nails and pretend it didn't matter. "Nope," I answered, simply because there was really nothing else to say.

"You okay with that?"

"Nothing I can do."

"You could talk to him about. Tell him how you feel."

I sat up and leaned my head on the driver's seat. "Then what? We're eighteen. We have our whole lives ahead of us. I'd rather keep him as a friend forever than a boyfriend for a little while."

"So you're willing to watch him be with other girls? What if he finds someone who's willing to tell him how she feels?" Ouch.

"It's not like I want to see him with other girls," I argued with a frown.

"Then do something about it. He's a foregone conclusion, Reagan."

I thought about it for a second. "No."

"Why not?"

"Because I don't want the easy choice. I don't want him to be with me in ten years because it's all we know, and I don't want him only because I don't want him to be with anyone else. He's not a toy in the sandbox." People who found each other young didn't stay happy together forever. They usually broke up at some point, sometimes for a short time and sometimes for forever. If we ever got together, I wanted us to be ready for a real future together.

She snorted. "And there is no chance it could be mutual and lasting now."

I ignored her. "Besides, it's not worth ruining everything. Everything's great how it is," I lied to get her off my back.

If I were forced to admit why I hid my feelings, fear would be the primary reason. A gun would likely have to be pointed at my head for me to fess up that little nugget. Even then I would probably be more afraid of the truth than the gun. Every time I considered telling Brock how I felt about him, doubts filled my mind. There were times when the words rested on my tongue, but I bit down on that stupid muscle to prevent it from releasing such ridiculous thoughts that could never be taken back. Because at the end of the day, it would hurt so much more if he didn't feel the same way. I could handle not knowing how he felt. Him breaking my heart was a completely different story.

Ivy obviously didn't understand what this was like. "Sometimes I think you're a boy." She fell back against her seat, exasperated with me.

I wasn't offended. In fact, I laughed and said, "That's okay. Sometimes I think you're a bitch."

She air-kissed me with a loud smack. Our friendship was weird.

"What about you and Neal?" Payback time.

"What about us?"

"What's up with you two? The tension is palpable."

"Pssh. There's nothing between us. The only reason he and I are friends is because of you and your friend, Brock. Besides, he's always liked another girl, but she's always been…preoccupied."

"Yeah. Whatever. I've seen you two cuddled up."

"Shut up." The conversation ended as the boys came back to the car laughing.

A sleeve of Chewy SweeTARTs came flying my way as soon as Brock opened the door. "What are these for?"

"They're your favorite." He shrugged.

Neal dramatically rolled his eyes and climbed in the driver's seat. I ignored him and caught Ivy raising an eyebrow in the side mirror. I shook my head, knowing exactly what she was thinking. It was not a sign of true love that he bought me my favorite candy, but then again, I knew people who settled for less. At least I would always have sugar highs to look forward to.

# Chapter Seven

### *Now*

Meyer didn't even make it through the first movie. She finished her bowl of ice cream and promptly fell asleep on Zoe's leg. Zoe failed to finish her ice cream, which made it perfectly clear that she did not share the same gene pool as Meyer and me. No member of the Anders family tree misses a chance to ingest sugar.

I ended up watching the entire Anne of Green Gables series and finishing the rest of the ice cream. Then I couldn't sleep because my stomach hurt so badly. I couldn't decide if it was because of the ungodly amount of sugar I had eaten that night or the reappearance of Brock in my life. Either way, my stomach churned while my mind flipped between playing Brock's words over and over again and my father's bad omen, "You only cross paths with people from your past who were really meant to be in your life."

While I considered it karma coming back to bite

me, my father used it as an excuse to ditch his family. All I wanted to do was wipe my brain clean of the memories that plagued me in the dark. I remembered everything about Brock, every detail that led up to me leaving. The memories were my motivation to put him behind me, but they were also the reason I couldn't.

Then he had the nerve to say, "I can't forget about you." Those were his last words before he drove off. What did that even mean? Had he been thinking about me this whole time like I thought about him? Or did he just want the closure that Jordan thought I needed? I was more confused than ever and feeling slightly hung over even though I hadn't had a drop of alcohol.

The next morning, I opened the store without my usual gusto. I didn't bother watching for Restaurant Guy to go to his car to strip out of his wetsuit. My mind was too preoccupied to enjoy the show. The shipment of books arrived, and I wasn't interested in ripping into the boxes like I usually did as soon as the delivery man set them down. This was why I didn't need him in my life. I spent all morning trying to decipher the meaning of his words instead of floating on my awesome cloud. I was already obsessing, and it had been one day.

Thankfully, Melanie showed up around lunchtime with BLTs and sweet potato chips. It was a random, delicious combination that could have only come from one place.

"Restaurant Guy asked about you," she said as she dropped the bags on the counter.

"Why?" I sounded far more disgusted than

confused, but I wasn't disgusted. I was weirded out. Why would a guy I periodically waved at ask about me? And why was another guy unable to forget about me?

"He said you weren't in the window this morning. He thought you might be sick."

"Nope. Not sick."

"So, why didn't you participate in your little game of wave and wink?"

"I've been busy."

She glanced around the store, taking in the boxes of books and the flashing light on the phone telling me I had messages. "I see that."

"Stop judging."

She held up her hands in surrender. "Not judging. More curious. What has the invincible Reagan all shook up?"

"Really, Melanie? Quoting Elvis?"

"Don't be cruel. Tell me what's up."

"That was lame."

"You're lame," she argued back.

This conversation was going nowhere fast, much like every other conversation we had. This was why I liked Melanie. She was always fun and never too serious. I also didn't think for a second that she would have ever invited Brock over to dinner or hired him to work with her...unlike my supposedly loyal brother.

"Are you going to tell me, or am I going to have to withhold the cheesecake Restaurant Guy sent?"

Ugh. I didn't think my stomach could take more, but as it turned out, the mention of cheesecake had my tongue snapping to attention.

"Jordan's kicking me out," I attempted to distract her.

"Not going to work. Sorry to hear that, but it's about time. Get back to the guy."

Double damn.

"My past is coming back to haunt me, and Casper is not a friendly ghost."

"Sounds intriguing. Tell me everything."

I debated keeping my mouth shut, but she would only badger me until I told her. Not to mention, I didn't have a single customer to distract me, or anywhere to be since she brought me lunch. She was a clever one, that Melanie.

"The guy I hung out with in high school and college has made a reappearance thanks to Jordan. We didn't end on good terms…or have an ending at all, really. We were sort of together when I was in an accident. The next morning, after I had been released from the hospital, my mom drove me back to the apartment. Right as we pulled into the · parking lot, he was walking out of his place with this leggy blonde bitch, Candace, in tow. That was the end. After that, I had to go home to recover from the accident, and I stopped speaking to him once I was gone." That was all she was getting as a brief overview of my history with Brock. When I finished, she remained silent for a long moment. Our food rested on the counter untouched, and my stomach hurt a little more after remembering all that happened.

"Say something."

"I just have one question."

"Okay…"

"What happened to the leggy blonde bitch?"

"Candace Wood?"

"Sure."

"Who knows? I wasn't aware of what Brock had been up to until last night."

"Really? You didn't once stalk him online?"

"No. I have the self-control of a monk."

"I'll say. I stalk the crap out of my exes. My high school boyfriend is balding and married to a woman who posts pictures of her kids eating constantly. He stopped being interesting years ago, but I can't seem to stop keeping tabs on him."

"You realize that's creepy, right?"

"You realize you're going to have to talk to him, right?"

"I thought you were going to be on my side. What good are you?"

"Hey! I brought you lunch."

"True. And cheesecake. Hand it over." I waved my hand, and she passed me the box of cherry-covered deliciousness.

After lunch I felt motivated to at least put the new shipment away, check the voicemail, and go through the book requests I still had to order. I stayed busy until closing then forced myself to run off some of the calories I had recently ingested. After a long soak in the tub, I fell into my bed and crashed for twelve hours straight.

The next morning I was in a better mood and even watched for Restaurant Guy to strip in the parking lot. His smile lit up his face when he saw me watching, and in a daring move, I actually winked at him. It was smoother than I would have predicted. Go me.

When I stepped back in the store, I literally patted myself on the back for my awesome moment, then scolded myself for doing such a lame thing as patting my own back. When would I ever learn?

Meyer showed up after school. She had spent Sunday hiding out in her room, so I was glad to see her in better spirits. After she added three more books to the waiting list, she took over the seat in the big bay window to conquer her latest obsession with another dystopian series.

I was busy calling customers to let them know their books had arrived when I heard the bell jingle over the door. People were in and out all the time, most of them browsers, so I didn't think anything of it until I heard Meyer snap, "What are you staring at?"

A low chuckle vibrated through the store, and I immediately knew who had entered. "You know, Reagan said the same thing to me the first time I met her."

"Then perhaps you should stop staring at people," Meyer told him.

"I just can't believe how much you look like her."

"Yeah, yeah. Get in line. No one can."

"What are you doing here?" I asked Brock without looking up from highlighting another name on the list. The less eye contact made, the better.

"Stopping by to see you. Waverly's, huh? Clever." Out of the corner of my eye, I saw him approaching the front where I was safely trapped behind the heavy wood and glass display.

"She was a great teacher."

"That she was." He crossed his arms and leaned against the counter, so all I could see were the muscles and his face that had girls doing double takes for years. "Who else would have put up with you challenging them every day like that?"

My eyes finally met his, and I found them full of humor and so familiar that it was hard to breathe. "No one, likely. That's why it was so fun. Now, why are you really here?"

"I was hoping I could take you to dinner. I think we should talk on more neutral ground."

"I can't tonight. I'm busy."

"You any good at scrabble?" Meyer interrupted, ignoring my scowl.

"The best. I used to beat her all the time," Brock nodded his head my way.

"Liar," I coughed out.

"Please," he scoffed. "I still hold the record from that game that lasted through the flood of 2001." Damn it. Did he forget anything?

Out of the corner of my eye, I saw Meyer's eyes flick between Brock and me. I knew what was coming before she opened her silly little mouth. "Why don't you come over? We're just having pizza and playing board games. We do it every Sunday night."

"Meyer, go call your dad." Her jaw dropped, and she did that teenager thing where she stomped her foot then stormed away when she saw I was serious. She was only ten! Since when do ten-year-olds act like that?

"So, I'll see you tonight." Brock turned and

stepped toward the door.

"What? No. That invitation doesn't count."

"Then come to dinner with me. It's one or the other, Rea." The nickname. He had me, and he knew it. Either he came to the house where everyone would be witness to the awkward tension between us or we had dinner alone. What was the lesser of the two evils?

"Fine. I'll join you for dinner." I decided keeping Jordan from having additional ammunition was worse than being alone with Brock then immediately regretted it.

"Good. Wear something casual," he said, then left the way he came, leaving me feeling dumbfounded...again.

"I'm not changing," I yelled after him. All my good feelings from this morning were gone. Since when do men want to talk?

# Chapter Eight

## *October 2001*

Where Ivy and I were attempting to take our freshman year seriously, college was all about partying and having a good time for Brock and Neal. They started going out a lot more as they made friends in their dorm. Ivy and I went with them sometimes, but I was an English major and with that came a ton of reading and even more papers to write. Ivy was pre-med, so she studied every second she could. People didn't realize Ivy was destined to be a surgeon. She could name all of the parts of the body in alphabetical order and their functions without batting an eye, but people always underestimated her intelligence because her bleach blonde hair, perfect heart-shaped face, and keen fashion sense. She was anything but stereotypical, and she worked hard to keep it that way. The library should have permanently etched our names on one of them with the amount of time we spent there our first few semesters.

The boys, on the other hand, didn't seem to take any of their classes seriously. Brock was always really good at math, so he was fine skipping those and doing the bare minimum. His literature class? Not so much. That's how he ended up joining us in the library, begging me to tutor him.

"Please, Rea!" he was on his knees. No joke. He was pleading with me in the middle of the library while Ivy took pictures and laughed at him. I wondered how long he would keep it up if I ignored him. "If I fail, I'll have to take it again." We were going on ten minutes and six people hushing him.

I glanced around the room and noticed people from the floor above us were leaning over the balcony, staring. It was time to end the charade. "Fine. Get up, loser."

"Thank you." He gave me a kiss on the cheek and pulled out a pack of Chewy SweeTARTs.

I laughed as I caught them mid-air. "You thought I was going to say no, didn't you?"

"No, but I never know for sure what you're going to do."

Aaannnd, I'm ignoring that. "Leave your shit. I'm hungry. You're buying me dinner first."

"Can't we study back at the dorm? This place gives me the creeps."

Sit on the bed and study with him like we did in high school? Nope. Not going to happen. We were returning to the safety of the library. "No." He groaned like an overgrown toddler but set his stuff down like a good little boy.

On our third night in a row at the library, I was happily chewing on my candy when he threw the book across the table. "How am I supposed to read this crap?"

I swallowed the sweet and tart candy too soon, making my eyes water. After I choked down some water, I sputtered, "It's the Canterbury Tales, Brock," as if that explained how to read Middle English. "This part's about a drunk guy. You should enjoy it."

"Ha. Ha. You're hilarious."

"I think so," I agreed with a shrug.

His hands dove into his hair, showing me just how much his arm muscles had changed. When did his biceps become so...hot?

"It's impossible," he groaned, forcing me to stop staring at his arms and focus again on his distress. "Why do I need to know this?"

"Because your professor said so." I slid the book on the table right in front of his face. He quickly adjusted his stance so he could see what I was about to show him. I didn't notice right away that I kept my arm looped my arm around his or that I rested my chin on his muscular arm. It was natural to lean on him like he was an extension of me, and his larger-than-the-average-bear biceps made excellent pillows. "It was written in the 14th century. It's cool that we even have access to it." The disgruntled look on his face made me laugh. "Remember when Mrs. Waverly made us read Beowulf?"

"Yeah. They killed the monster and its mom, then they all got drunk."

"That was in Old English, and you understood that."

"I had a great study partner." He looked down at

me with a sweet smile. That was the moment I realized how close we were to kissing. Our noses were almost touching. We were both smiling. It was another picturesque moment that was just as fleeting as all the other good times we had shared.

"Brock?"

We both looked up to see a familiar face in front of us of whom I only had bad memories. Her presence had me quickly pulling away from Brock and regretting the tinge of hope I had felt moments before. Candace Wood stood tall, looking like she had just finished a photo shoot. Seriously, who wore high heels to the library?

"I thought that was you."

"Candace? What are you doing here?"

"UCLA didn't work out." She waved it off as if it was unimportant, giving me the distinct impression it was a story I would very much like to hear.

"Oh," Brock responded in a way that indicated he was interested in her sudden appearance. That was enough for me. I didn't need to hear or see anymore. They could have a reunion fuck on the library table for all I cared. I just didn't want to witness to it.

"All righty. I'm out. Good luck on your paper, Brock."

"Where are you going?"

"Work." Brock knew I didn't have to be at my part time job at a local bookstore until much later, but he didn't challenge me. I waited a moment more for him to say something. Instead his eyes flicked between mine, then looked away, so I grabbed my stuff and walked out…again.

From that point on, our little tutoring sessions were bland and straightforward. He noticed. I noticed. I think everyone in the library noticed.

During a discussion of The Odyssey, he turned to look me in the eyes. "Why have you been acting weird?"

"I'm not acting weird!" I had totally been acting weird.

He raised his eyebrows, giving me a challenging look. I frowned back at him, annoyed that he caught on to me pouting since Candace, the slut, made her reappearance.

"Fine. If you don't want to admit it now, you don't have to, but eventually you'll tell me what's up."

"Whatever," I muttered before turning back to my books.

"Reagan, I've spent more time with you than any other human being in the world, and you still can't just say what's on your mind."

"Says he who can't say the word 'feelings' without cringing."

"Oh, I can say it. I feel very strongly that if you don't just tell me what's wrong, I'm going to throw you down on this table and tickle you until you pee all over yourself."

"You wouldn't."

He moved closer, so close that the only thing I could see were his brown eyes. "I would, and you know it."

"This isn't high school anymore. People actually come to the library because they care about their school work."

He laughed then, went quiet with a faraway look in his eyes. When that smile reserved only for memories with me covered his face, I knew he was remembering the time Mrs. Waverly caught us doing naughty things in the back of our high school library.

"Poor Mrs. Waverly." He grinned, and I knew that any attempt he had made at talking about what was on my mind was gone. We were just Brock and Reagan again.

I laughed then agreed. "Poor Mrs. Waverly."

That was the moment, the turning point. We started hanging out again like the old days. Neal seemed to be busy. Ivy was working in a lab. Candace was noticeably and thankfully absent. The partying seemed to take a backseat unless the four of us went out, but more often than not, Brock and I were together. At night we fell asleep together watching movies, and during the day we would study or run or whatever we wanted to do. The world was our oyster…until it wasn't.

Neal started showing up more and more when Brock and I were together. Our bliss was first interrupted with the comment, "Why don't you just fuck her?" Brock's head snapped up, and his expression looked like he was going to climb over the table and choke Neal, but he did nothing. He didn't say a word or make any violent threats. Honestly, I was hoping for the latter. I couldn't say I didn't consider punching him myself, but I was too busy feeling disappointed in Brock for not standing up for us.

Neal's comments didn't stop. It was either something crude or constant questions about how we could possibly be "just" friends. It was all very reminiscent of the way Ivy used to challenge me about Brock back in high school. Ivy used to at least ask questions in private. Now Neal had jumped on the bandwagon without any discretion, and I didn't like it one bit. Brock eventually started to tell Neal to fuck off, but the more Neal showed up, the more Brock pulled away from me. It was the first time that had happened.

To make matters worse, I was a little hurt...okay, a lot hurt...that Brock's partying picked up shortly after Neal's comments started. I knew it was my fault. I pushed him away again, but did he have to take it out on every poor unsuspecting blonde girl on campus? It was made worse by the fact that he wanted me to meet all of his charming concubines. After the third time he introduced me as "the girl you've got to impress," I was done.

Girl number three was a pretty blonde. She wore a lot of mascara and little clothing. I didn't fault her for her choice in attire. She had a kickin' body, so why not? She was tall enough to kiss him on the cheek without him having to bend over. Basically, she was the opposite of me. I had long, curly brown hair, only hit five and a half feet in heels, and didn't feel the need to glam out to hang out at someone's apartment and drink beer. Blondies one, two, and three were all glam girls. They were three more versions of Candace.

"This is my best friend and the girl you need to

impress," Brock told her. "She says no, then you're a no go."

She giggled and slapped his chest, probably thinking he was kidding. He sounded like he was joking, but his eyes told me he wasn't. Part of me wondered if this was his way of challenging me. These girls were harmless. They weren't what Brock would want in the long run. He knew it too. That's why he picked them. The one thing I wasn't sure about was whether or not he wanted me to say no to her. Was it wishful thinking that it appeared he wanted me to stop him? It had to be. Even though I felt him trying to silently communicate to me, for the first time ever, I couldn't figure out what it was.

I went with not looking like the jealous harpy. "She's pretty. Have fun, Brock." I patted his shoulder as I walked by and didn't look back. Ivy and I were at our dorm with ice cream and movies within twenty minutes. If you asked Ivy, she would say nothing Brock did affected me. We played "would you rather" until I distracted her with gummy bears and Richard Gere. I laughed and joked while we analyzed the merits of Pretty Woman as the premise for a reality TV show. Not even my own mother would have known that all I could think about was what Brock was doing with Blondie.

Brock showed up the next morning with orange juice and donut holes. He knew it was my favorite breakfast combination. As she headed out to class, Ivy gave me a look that indicated she figured more was going on the night before than I had let on. As soon as the door closed, Brock was climbing onto my bed and handing me chocolate donuts.

"What's this for?" I asked with my mouth full and not even an ounce of regret at being so unladylike.

"Just wanted to hang out." He shrugged and threw a blueberry donut hole into his mouth.

"How was your night last night?"

He turned his head to stare at me for a moment. I shoved another donut hole in my mouth and refused to acknowledge him. I didn't want him to see the hurt that lingered underneath the surface. He must have anyway—and here I thought sugar made everything better. Silly me.

"You know she meant nothing, right?"

"Yeah…sure," I replied brightly and hid the lie with more food. At this rate I was going to eat all of them by myself. "Nothing but a warm body, right?" I joked with a wink, trying too hard to joke. I felt like an ass.

Brock wasn't in a playful mood this fine morning. "You can always say no if you don't like a girl I meet." Did he seriously want to talk about this?

"Pssh. It's not like I had a chance to get to know her. You didn't know her."

"Yeah. I didn't really need to know her."

I waited for him to elaborate. Of course he didn't. I guess I didn't really want him to tell me more anyway. Seconds passed where I could practically hear him say the words that rested on the tip of his tongue, so I finally had to ask, "What do you mean?"

He swallowed some juice and stared into space. "We can't always get what we want," he muttered cryptically.

"Seems that way," I agreed, feeling confused as to what we were really talking about and a little broken because he was oh-so-right.

# Chapter Nine

## *Now*

"Reagan. So not cool," Damien called out as he and his girlfriend, Kira, plopped onto stools at the front desk of my store. It was almost closing time, almost time for Brock to meet me for dinner, and I was a nervous wreck. Damien and Kira were the perfect distraction.

Last year, when I first met Damien Rush, he hadn't read a book since elementary school. Even then I was sure that the only books he had read were actually read aloud to him. Now he read anything and everything I could give him and his writing was inspiring in its own regard. This kid, who I met picking up trash outside my store as part of his community service, had not only come a long way, but he was insightful and creative. I enjoyed having him as my friend and reading buddy.

"For real, Reagan," Kira agreed. "That is, like, the saddest book. Why in the world would you have us read that?"

"Did you take anything away from it?"

"You know we did." Damien grinned and patted his well-loved copy of Tuesdays with Morrie.

"Then let's discuss."

By the time Brock arrived to pick me up, the three of us had tears in our eyes, even Damien. I loved these moments. A lot of high school kids hung out in my store. So many of them had never appreciated the love of a good book until someone showed them the one that hooked them. I enjoyed being the crazy bookstore lady that introduced them to a passion for reading. I was supposed to be closing up but allowed myself to enjoy the distraction only Damien and Kira provided. He took in the three of us, perplexed by the way we were wiping our eyes and laughing.

"Damien, Kira, this is an old friend, Brock." They greeted him when he offered his hand to shake.

"You guys okay?" he asked us, and Kira explained about the book. When Brock saw the cover, he understood. I had once made him read it as well.

"Great book," he commented, then remained quiet while Kira and Damien finished telling me their favorite quotes.

Once they had left us alone, Brock watched me close out the register and prepare the deposit before he said, "I never pictured you running your own business, but a bookstore suits you."

I thought about all the trouble I had finding a career. Brock had always teased me about majoring in "reading," but there was nothing else I wanted to do forever. It turned out there really were very few jobs for an English major. "It was Jordan's idea. I guess you were right. There was really nothing out there for me. I couldn't commit to anything."

"Or anyone?" I would have thought it was an insult had it not been phrased like a question.

"Or anyone," I confirmed quietly.

He sucked in a deep breath and let it out. "Come on. Let's feed you. You can even get dessert if you want."

I gave him a look that said, "Are you crazy?" making him throw his head back and laugh out loud. "I see sugar is still your favorite."

"The only reason I eat anything else is so I can have more sweets."

His laughter didn't fade as he followed me out of the store. I locked up, then turned to him. It was then that I noticed how nice he looked in black pants and a blue dress shirt with the sleeves rolled up. Blue was a good color on him, and seeing him dressed like this made me realize he was a grown up now. When did we grow up? I still felt like a kid most of the time. I looked down at my casual tea dress and matching Converse shoes and squirmed a bit. I suddenly felt embarrassed by my immaturity.

"You okay?" he asked.

I ignored his question because I didn't know the answer. "Where to?"

"There's a place right down here that I heard is pretty good." He pointed to Restaurant Guy's place, and I frowned. I didn't want to show up at Restaurant Guy's with Brock. I didn't want to go there with anyone. Restaurant Guy was still the highlight of my day. No need to ruin it.

"Or not," Brock added when he saw my face. "You know this area better than I do."

I smiled. "I have just the spot."

I led him down the boardwalk past the parking lot to a place that I usually avoided. It was a family-owned joint decorated with antiques from all over the US. They served fresh seafood and the best crab soup I had ever tasted. It reminded me of this dive Brock and I used to go whenever we went to the beach for cheap seafood. He was the reason I never ate at the place, but since I would be sitting across the table from him, I figured no sense in skipping out on the delicious crab soup tonight. I'd had it once before and always wanted to come back for it, but the atmosphere brought back too many memories. I settled for avoiding the place instead. But since I was here…

"This looks just like—"

"I know," I interrupted. "I figured you'd like it. The crab soup is the best in the world. Really. They should advertise it as such."

He was awestruck taking everything in. "It's uncanny how similar it is. Are you sure it isn't the same owners?"

A young girl seated us, then took our drink order before scurrying away.

"A guy named Darryl and his wife Barbara own this place. She reads erotic romances, and he likes to read books on how to fix things even though Barbara refuses to let him 'handyman' in her house. Her words."

"You know these people?"

When the waitress returned with our drinks, she took our order for the soup and a platter Brock thought looked good for us to share. I didn't mind him ordering for us. Even after all this time he still knew what I liked—but I couldn't think about that right then.

"I know almost everyone who works around here. This is a pretty small town."

"Yeah, I know. I like it. Good surf, nice people. I was lucky to find a job here."

"How did you? Specifically, how did you end up working with Jordan?"

"Truth?"

I nodded. "It's too much of a coincidence for you to simply land there, so yes, I would like the truth."

"Okay, but you have to promise to stick around after I tell you, so we can have some of the world's best soup."

"Fine."

"And you have to give me something in return."

"What?"

"A truth of your own."

I sunk back in my chair and asked, "What do you want to know?" I had an idea, but you never could never be sure with Brock.

"Just agree, then we'll truth it up."

The waitress delivered the soup and the platter all at the same time, and I took a moment to think while she set it in front on us. Did I want to know how he came to work with Jordan? Couldn't I just ask Jordan? He hadn't told me anything so far.

"No. Jordan won't tell you."

I glanced up with the question written on my

face.

"I can read your mind. You're trying to find a way out of the deal. It won't work. Jordan won't tell you anything."

"How do you know?"

"He agreed not to. He wants you to talk to me just as much as I do."

Screw my damn brother. "Fine, but you go first."

"Of course. I met Jordan last year at a conference. The last name stuck out to me. I told him I once knew a girl with the same name. Over drinks, I briefly shared my tragic story about the one who got away. The whole time he said nothing."

I wondered how much he told Jordan. He had known about Brock. The first night I stayed at his house we drank tequila and attempted to get to know each other by asking what started out as simple questions. The questions became progressively deeper, and I was too drunk to filter. I wasn't sure how much Jordan understood, so was it possible that he would he have made the connection?

"The following week I received a phone call from Jordan's company about consulting work. I was later paired up with Jordan on a small project, and when he flew to Seattle to wrap it up, he confessed that he was your brother. He spent the year trying to decide if he should let me back in your life. Sure enough, when a position opened within his company, I was the first person they called."

"So, it was all planned."

"Sort of. We both figured you wouldn't see me or speak to me, but I still can't figure out why. What happened, Rea?"

"Is that your one truth you want from me?"

"No."

"What do you want to know?"

His eyes met mine and bored into me like he was unsure about what he was about to say. Just as quickly as I saw the nerves, they were gone and confidence had taken over him.

"What?" I asked, prompting him to finally speak.

"Were you ever in love with me?"

I choked on the hot soup. Sputtering, I coughed out, "What?"

"You heard me. I want to know if you ever loved me, because I sure as hell was head over heels in love with you, but then you left, and I..." He paused. "Let's just say that was a feeling I'll never forget."

I coughed more, breaking up the leftover soup that went down the wrong tube.

"You promised me a truth, Reagan, and that's what I want to know."

My heart pounded. I could feel the blood rushing through my body. I knew my cheeks were red, and my ears burned. That was not a question I expected at all, but I had promised him a truth, and I always kept my promises.

"Yes," I whispered to the seafood platter. I couldn't bear to look him in the eye when I said the words I had never spoken aloud, especially not to him. "Yes, I loved you."

# Chapter Ten

## *March 2002*

There's a feeling of power, a high if you will, when someone cares enough about you to protect you. That was definitely not what this was, and the feeling I was left with was nothing like a high. In fact, what I felt wasn't even remotely satisfying.

Ivy and I went to a party hosted by some guy she met in her biology class. Alex was older and "sooo hot," so I was dressed in the heeled boots, skinny jeans, and low-cut top she picked out as I followed her into his house. He apparently shared it with three other guys and had people over every weekend. I could already tell it was going to be a long and possibly painful night.

Two beers in, I was bored, and my feet hurt. I had seen a guy drink a beer from a funnel followed by a girl who didn't shave her armpits doing a keg stand. I watched people bump and grind on the makeshift dance floor and witnessed a couple practically having sex on the couch in the middle of the room, not even in a dark corner. All the while Ivy was flirting with the mildly attractive guy known as Alex. I had sporadically chatted with one of his roommates, who was cute but boring. He asked every possible question he could about me, and I responded with variations of, "What about you?" Lame, I know.

When I was finishing my drink, he was on his fifth or tenth. Who knew? This was when the compliments started. "You're so beautiful," he said and looked longingly at me. Uhm...awkward much? He followed up with, "Those boots make you look hot, and your shirt is sexy as fuck." Yuck. Then he added, "We should go out sometime," while slipping his arm around my waist.

"I don't think so, buddy. I hardly know you."

"You could get to know me," he slurred.

I didn't have a chance to answer him. A very angry Brock marched right up to us and spoke quietly, making his presence more menacing than if he had yelled. "Take your hands off her."

"We're talking. Back off." The idiot made a mistake pushing Brock. He had gotten in fights for less in high school, and this time was no different.

Brock took the guy's hand and twisted it behind his back. "Take your hand off her or I break this one."

"Fine, man." The guy surrendered and started to walk away. "She was a bitch anyway."

"Oh crap," I muttered, knowing what was coming.

Brock spun around and shouted, "What did you just call her?"

I wasn't offended, but I knew Brock was about to lose it. He had always been protective of me. Sure enough, when the dumbass repeated himself, Brock didn't hesitate to throw a right hook right into his jaw. When he tried to tackle Brock, the guy ended up in a headlock while Brock took a few more shots to his abdomen. A crowd surrounded us now, and people were yelling from all directions.

"Fight! Fight!"

The girls were squealing, and I stood frozen. I was trapped in a corner with no escape. I realized this wasn't going to end well, and I yelled. "Stop!" It didn't help.

Alex busted through the crowd and pulled his friend back. When they split apart enough, I snuck in and flattened my palms on Brock's chest. He was breathing heavily, and his corded muscles were tense and flexed.

"Stop, Brock. Stop."

Finally, his eyes made contact with mine. They widened in realization just before he hugged me against him. "You okay, Rea?"

"I'm fine. You're the one fighting."

He laughed.

"You need to get out of here, man," Alex shouted.

Brock held up his hands and said, "No problem." Guiding me by the small of my back, he led us out the front door while we laughed at his typical antics. He turned me and held my face between his palms. "You okay, Rea?" This time when he said the words, they felt different. He spoke softly and looked in my eyes like he was trying to say so much more, or maybe that was wishful thinking.

I was certain we were home free. The way he was looking at me was so intimate that I almost said something I would later regret. Instead I said, "Thank you," hoping he would understand what I really wanted to say. He barely nodded, and I knew he was going to kiss me. He was so close, but a pretty blonde girl came bouncing down the steps calling, "Brock," in a high-pitched voice that would have dogs howling. The second her squeal interrupted the moment I was pulling away. He quickly let me go when she cried, "Oh my god! Are you okay? What happened? Why did you hit that guy?"

The girl looked him over familiarly. Then, to my horror, she kissed him, and he kissed her back. "I'm fine, Jennie. Everything's okay."

"Jennie?" I asked before my brain knew what my mouth was doing.

"Yeah, Jennie. This is Reagan, my best friend." He kept talking, but I didn't hear what he said. I was placed firmly in the friend zone. I kind of knew that might have been the case, but the silly girl inside of me was still holding onto the hope that he was pining for what we used to have like I had been.

Ivy came running out of the house next, asking what happened. She told me Alex was boring, so we left Brock with his date to get ice cream. I was doomed to face hours of questions about Brock before I could go to sleep that night if I didn't think of something fast. Instead of allowing her to ask anything other than Cherry Garcia or Strawberry

Cheesecake, I put Ivy under the microscope and spit out every possible asinine question about her night with Alex. He really was the most boring human on the planet.

Then something weird happened, something I could have never predicted. Ivy and Neal started dating for real. I had no idea they were even hanging out until I skipped class one day. Don't judge. It was geology, which was a dumb class. Why I chose to study rocks for even a semester was beyond me.

When I walked in my dorm room that day, the last thing I expected to see was Neal's bare ass doing the dirty with my roomie. I opened the door, not even paying attention to what was going on around me. I almost made it to my bed when I saw a butt, a naked butt. I screamed and attempted to back out but I ran into the wall. I covered my eyes and apologized as I used the wall to guide my way out of the room. The next thing I knew, I was sitting in the hall on my knees and laughing hysterically. I'm sure my neighbors thought I was insane, but if they had just seen the smiley face tattoo on their roommate's boyfriend's ass, they might have felt a little nutty too.

Ivy told me everything. He asked her out after our road trip. She didn't know he meant it as a date, but it ended up being the best date she'd ever been on. They stayed up talking all night and found they had a lot in common. She said the conversation was "deep" and that he "understood the darkest parts of her." I wondered what she meant but didn't ask. I never shared my dark parts with her, so I wasn't going to ask about hers.

Apparently Neal did ask…they kept their relationship going privately, much like Brock and I tried to do in high school. It seemed they talked about everything over the past couple of years, but they didn't actually decide to be together until recently. Neal was why she ditched Alex so abruptly after making such a point to let everyone know how hot he was, which he wasn't. She was trying to make Neal jealous to force him to make a move. It worked. She said she liked being with him…a lot. What she didn't say was that she liked him, but that was Ivy for you.

Brock laughed when I told him what happened. Neal would never live down the smiley face tattoo now that I knew he had it done because he lost a bet to Brock. Anytime we could bring up "smiley ass," we made sure to do just that. I think it only fueled Neal's dislike of me, but a smiley! On his rear! Who could resist?

"That reminds me," Brock said after explaining about Neal's hidden smiley, "you never showed me your tattoo."

"And I can't now. It's not the kind of thing you show off in public." We were in a Starbucks. It wasn't like I'd have to show off like a porn star, but the tattoo wasn't something I needed to show him in front of others.

"Aren't you a little minx?" he teased.

He had no idea. I wasn't hiding it to tease him. I was keeping it to myself because I feared he wouldn't understand.

"You wanna do something this weekend? Just

the two of us like old times?"

"How much like old times?" I asked, wondering if he was proposing hanging out as friends or friends with benefits. It sounded like dear ol' Jennie was out of the picture, and I was ready to have my Brock back. Maybe jealousy worked on me as well.

"Like we do something fun. Drive down to the beach?"

"Sure." And so we did. We went to our favorite beach, played in the ocean, walked the shore, took silly pictures on the boardwalk, and drove back to school. It was the best day I'd had in a long time. No serious talks took place. It was just him and me being us.

He loved it as much as I did. I know he did, but when we were back at school, it was like the day never happened. The four of us went out a few nights later, and guess who showed her pretty little face? Yup. Jennie, Brock's latest pretty blonde girl. It was a super fun night, especially the part when she and Brock went home together. Then Ivy went home with Neal, and I went back to my dorm alone. No ice cream and movie to keep me company this time. I needed something more depressing, so I focused on my readings from Dostoyevsky.

When Jennie appeared again and again with Brock, I was forced to face the fact that he had a girlfriend. She was nice. That was really all I had to say about her. Needless to say, I didn't see her much. All my friends were part of couples, and I wasn't one to be the fifth wheel. I found other ways to keep myself busy. At first I kept company with Aristotle, Homer, Sophocles, and Plato. Then I made friends with a few people in my history class who studied by watching inaccurate movies of historical events. Finally, I decided it was my turn to have a little fun.

The only thing that made my geology class even remotely interesting was the teaching assistant, Wesley Boyd. He was cute in a geeky kind of way. I loved how passionate he was about rocks. When he led an erosion lab, I could see how environmental science could be exciting, sort of. Geology was something I would have complained to Brock about, no doubt, but he was too busy with Jennie. Yeah, I was a jealous harpy that had hurt feelings and maybe a broken heart. Stupid heart.

The reminder of Brock had me returning my focus to Wesley. As I listened to him discuss the process of weathering, I decided a little extra geology help wouldn't hurt, and Wesley was more than happy to help me. During our study session the next night, he said he had wanted to ask me out but couldn't. School policy didn't allow TAs to date students in their section. Thankfully he could still help me prepare for my finals, though. Our first kiss was when I accurately described the six characteristics of rocks and minerals without help. I may not be able to tell Dunite and Andesite apart, but I could bullshit my way through a short answer question and kiss a cute boy at the same time.

But I digress. Like I said, he was passionate about geology. The night before the final he seemed laser focused at first. Then things evolved into a less formal tutoring session. When I showed him I learned what he wanted, he seemed proud of me. He kept leaning closer and closer to me, and I mirrored him step for step as I listed each characteristic. He was cute and smart, and when we kissed, I could only describe it as nice, gentle, and sweet. His smile widened when we separated. I was sure mine matched his. I aced that final, and the second my grade was entered he called and asked me on a real date.

Ivy met Wes on a Wednesday. That Saturday I was being forced to go on a double date with my new dating buddy, my roommate, and her boyfriend, also known as Brock's best friend. I didn't start dating Wes to play tit for tat with Brock, so I didn't really want Neal to tell Brock about every move he made, but I couldn't say I wouldn't have been happy to have him stand outside my dorm with a boom box over his head playing some Dave Matthews or something. So, I counted the days until Brock came to see me. I waited and hoped he would come fight for my honor. He and Dave never made an appearance.

I ended things with Wes two weeks later.

According to Ivy, Jennie lasted another week.

# Chapter Eleven

### *Now*

I pushed my chair back, ready to bolt. I couldn't breathe, and I thought I might cry. I hated crying. I felt ashamed. I felt afraid. I felt a lot of uncomfortable emotions that I had been purposely avoiding for the last several years, and one dinner with Brock made me lose all sense of control. Everything was closing in on me. It was all too much.

His hand gently closed around my arm and held me down. "Breathe, Rea. It's okay. I felt the same. I'm pretty sure I still do. What we had isn't something you get over."

The tears started then, and I quickly used my napkin to stop them. This was so humiliating, crying in a restaurant. "We were awful to each other."

"Not always," he reminded me.

When I looked up, I saw the concern all over his perfect face. His strong jaw was slack, his eyes were wide, and he bit his lip like he did when he read something he wasn't sure about.

"This is pointless, Brock. We can never go back, and I'm not that girl anymore."

He smiled, showing me his relief and his perfect teeth. "I don't know about that. Why don't we finish eating, then go on a walk? I bet there's some of that girl left in you somewhere."

"I hope not."

"I hope so," he argued, "Because then I still know a piece of you, even if it's a small piece."

"When you realize I'm not the person you think I am, you might go running in the other direction."

"Reagan, knowing what I know now, I may never let you go."

We'll see about that, I thought but kept it to myself as he passed me a crab leg to tear into. Through the rest of dinner, we discussed safer topics like our moms and our jobs. He asked a lot of questions about Meyer, and I regaled him with funny stories of Jordan and I doing our brother-sister parenting thing.

"Where's her mom?"

"Gone. She gave up her rights the day Meyer was born and never looked back. She and Jordan were having a bit of fun. Meyer's mom never wanted kids, but stayed clean long enough to pop out a healthy baby."

"That's sad."

"I don't know. She would have made a terrible mom. I only met her a handful of times, but she was pretty rough around the edges. I think Meyer is lucky her mom let her go. It was almost like she loved her enough to let someone else raise her."

"You have changed," Brock commented thoughtfully.

"This I know."

"You were also so opinionated about parents leaving their kids."

"What my father did and what Meyer's mom did were two completely different things. Had my father left before I knew what it was like to have a two-parent home, I wouldn't have been so broken up about it. He also left to be with his other family. That was a tough pill to swallow."

"I couldn't agree more. Clarity looks good on you, Rea."

"Everything looks good on you, Brock. What have you been eating? Spinach?"

"You should have learned to surf. It does a body good."

"I see surfers all the time. None of them look like you." Except Restaurant Guy. Even though he was hot enough to be on the cover of a romance novel, he didn't hold a candle to Brock. There was just something about Brock's physical appearance that hit all the right buttons for me.

"Well, look all you want, Rea. You haven't changed a bit physically, which is shocking considering how much junk you eat, and I'm still liking what I see."

"Hmm, yes. Some things never change." I laughed. We were always physically attracted to each other. That was the one thing we had no trouble discussing.

I caught myself laughing more than once

throughout dinner, and I couldn't believe how quickly we fell into our old comfort. Really, I shouldn't have been surprised considering we were always like that. I had to be careful, though. I wasn't sure that was a trap I wanted to fall back into…or that I could handle.

We decided to walk on the beach and risk getting sand in unmentionable places even though we'd have our clothes on. Seriously, how did sand do that?

Brock rolled up his pants and slid his shoes and socks off while I did the same. We each carried our shoes, so it surprised me when he took my free hand in his. I wasn't a hundred percent sure how I felt about it, but I didn't pull away. So much of me enjoyed feeling his touch again, even if was just handholding. A smaller but no less significant part of me feared the hope I unwillingly felt. Hope was what led to bad decisions, but I still feared the way Brock made me feel wonderful and yet incredibly out of control.

"I'm glad you moved here," Brock said as we walked along the edge of the water.

"Why?"

"It's so peaceful. It's a nice contrast from how your brain works."

"I can't decide if that was an insult or you saying you care about my well-being."

"It wasn't an insult," he pointedly replied.

"I picked this town. Jordan and Meyer promised to follow when I found a place I wanted to be. Meyer was probably six when we arrived here. We drove through on the way to see my mom once. The three of us ate where we did tonight, then sat in our car in the parking lot eating ice cream and listening to the waves crashing. It was the only time in my life I wasn't thinking about the past or the future. I was completely in the moment, enjoying my strawberry ice cream."

"So, the three of you packed up and moved here?"

"Not right away. The closer we drove to home, the worse I started feeling. I hadn't known what it felt to be completely relaxed until I wasn't anymore."

"Why couldn't you relax?"

"Let's leave that for another day. Tell me about Adam. You said he's getting married."

"Yes, and she's perfect for him. I didn't think so at first because she left him, but she came back, and now they're happier than ever." Ouch. Yeah, I didn't miss the implication of his words. She came back, but you didn't.

Brock told me all about Katherine as we walked further down the beach, keeping my hand in his the whole way. In turn, I told him more about Zoe and Jordan. It was easier to talk about other people than us. It was even easier to keep the conversation going while looking ahead instead of at each other.

"Jordan said you think he's weird."

"Did he now?"

"Yes, that was his excuse for inviting you to dinner."

"Huh. Well, it is a little weird that he lives with his sister. He's been with Zoe awhile, and you should hear how he talks about her. Well, I suppose you might know better than I do, really."

"Yes, I think I'll be homeless soon. They might be getting close to taking the next step in their relationship."

"How would Meyer take you moving out?"

"As long as she could come to the store every day, she'd be okay. She's becoming more independent as she grows. She's extremely mature for her age, likely due to the fact she had two people who had no idea how to raise a kid teaching her everything."

Before I knew it, we were back at the parking lot. It was time to say goodbye. It was the last thing I wanted even if I knew it was for the best for my poor heart, my poor, very confused heart.

"I'm not ready to say goodbye," Brock admitted when we were standing next to my Hummer.

"No, but I think it's for the best for now. We can't keep sweeping everything under the rug and pretending the lumps aren't there. Eventually we're going to trip over them."

"I suppose so. Does that mean you're ready to tell me why you left?"

Talking about everything sounded like an awful idea, but I knew it was the only thing that would bring us to the present. He needed to know why I ran, and I needed to know why he made some of the choices he did. Then maybe I could let him go. Maybe we could be friends. Maybe I could date Restaurant Guy. Why did that suddenly sound so unappealing when he was the best part of my day only yesterday?

"Rea?" Brock prompted.

"Yeah, I think it's time to talk."

# Chapter Twelve

## *November 2002*

Ivy and Neal became closer while Brock and I pulled further apart. It frightened me to think we had ruined everything, that we'd never be the same. I couldn't even pinpoint the moment that it all went sour. Even though things weren't the way I had hoped, I constantly thought of him. Every book character I read was Brock. Every paper I wrote had an element of negativity that made every sentence a little pessimistic and dark. By the end of sophomore year, I was confused, lonely, and desperate to feel anything else but hurt.

The opportunity to fix things with Brock presented itself when Ivy and Neal decided we were all moving to apartments. I would still be living with Ivy. Neal and Brock would still live together, but we would all be in the same building. Part of me dreaded watching him parade his girls through our shared building, but I was still attempting to appear unfazed by his shenanigans and saw this as a chance to get close to him again.

The boys helped us move in when we promised to pay them in beer and pizza, as if it even took that to convince them to lift heavy furniture for us poor, helpless females, but it didn't go as I expected. Brock and I had next to no interaction. He did his part to set up our apartment, then bolted out of there like his pants were on fire. I was left with Ivy and Neal, rearranging the couch seventeen times until Ivy was happy with its placement. Neal didn't argue once and did whatever he could to make Ivy happy. I was officially the third wheel moving into my own apartment. The whole day was one huge disappointment considering how excited we were to be moving there.

After that first night, I hardly saw Ivy. She spent even less time in the apartment than she did the dorm. If she wasn't studying, she was with Neal. When she was there, she was lost in her own head, much like I was. I kept wondering why we bothered living together if we were hardly going to speak. My mom was calling twice a day because she was worried about me. My grades were fine, but I didn't do anything other than study and work my part-time job filing in the admissions office. There was nothing more mindless than filing papers in the admissions office. My life was depressing.

It occurred to me later that Ivy must have felt similar, maybe even worse, but we never spoke about it. It wasn't odd for me to come home from class to find her sitting alone in the dark. No television. No lights. Nothing. She once claimed she was sleeping, but no one sleeps sitting up like that.

It was weird, like everything else.

"You okay, Ivy?" I asked.

"Yeah, just worn out from Neal. Ugh, he can't get enough of me." She always said something along these lines, knowing I wouldn't ask for more information.

"Right..." I didn't need that picture. "What's up with sitting in the dark?"

"I don't know. It's peaceful." And wait for it... "You going to come out with us tonight? Get all dolled up, so Brock doesn't know what hit him?" There it is. The abrupt change of subject to Brock.

"No. If he wanted to hang out, we would."

"You're so blind."

"What does that mean?"

"He's waiting on you. You're waiting on him. All you two are ever going to do is wait on each other because neither of you has the balls to do anything about it."

"Not true."

"Isn't it?" she added sarcastically as she poured a bowl of cereal. I stood there frozen for a second, annoyed with Ivy, then myself for even acknowledging this line of thinking.

"Shut up," I said and escaped to the safety and loneliness of my room.

Eventually I decided I was tired of feeling like crap and being alone all the time. The one person who used to always make me laugh lived right upstairs, and I was done pushing him away.

So, what was I to do? I had to distract him from his blondes while ensuring I didn't seem as if I was throwing myself at him. I had my pride to think about, after all. I came up with a plan, and it involved pizza and chocolate cupcakes.

I "accidentally" gave the pizza place the wrong apartment number. Mine was 212, and his was 312, honest mistake. Since he and I both liked the same kind of pizza, I knew that was all it would take for him to personally escort that pizza to my apartment, where the chocolate cupcakes were lined up on the counter cooling while I mixed the icing. I had him hook, line, and sinker.

"Trying to master baking again, Rea?" he asked as he set the box down on the table.

It had taken me four boxes to get twelve delicious looking cupcakes. I went through three dozen eggs because I dropped a dozen on the stairs and screwed up so many cupcakes.

"I think I have it this time."

"Yeah, right."

"I swear it," I told him. "You can be the judge."

"Hmm…official taste tester of your baking," he thought aloud as he poked at a cupcake. "It's a dangerous job, but someone has to do it."

And just like that I had him for the night. He pulled out plates and served each of us pizza before he helped me ice and eat six cupcakes. The other six met their demise in the trashcan. I wasn't one to throw out perfectly good cake because of aesthetics, but when it tasted like chalk, it had to go. I wasn't even sure how that happened.

As much as I hated to admit it, Ivy was right about Brock wanting me back in his life. He seemed happy that things had gone back to normal. After the pizza guy offered the proverbial olive branch, he started showing up at my apartment every time Ivy was in his. Suddenly it was high school all over again. We still never discussed anything about the past, but I was so happy with the present that I didn't feel the need to acknowledge anything before it.

Everything was good, good, good. The whole tit for tat dating thing stopped, but only because we were always together. By Halloween we were in each other's bed again. By Thanksgiving it was every night, and by Christmas I decided it was time to confess how I felt about him. That made me a nervous wreck, but I swore to myself I would tell him before something else could happen that made me want to push him away again.

I gave myself a deadline to prepare my brain and my heart. The day before we went home for the holidays was the big day. Daddy issues be damned, the words would come out of my mouth come hell or high water. I was in love with Brock Anderson. He was it for me, no doubt. Any thoughts I had about young love had been eradicated by time spent with him, in and out of bed, and I told myself it was okay.

I needed a friend to back me up and wanted to talk to Ivy. I could imagine how she'd say, "Finally!" with exasperation, and it would be the push necessary to go through with it. I usually wasn't interested in girl talk before I did something, but I had never cared this much about anything before. As much as I hated it, the extra boost of confidence only a friend could provide would have been really helpful. Unfortunately, she wasn't around or with Neal. He came by looking for her. When I told him I hadn't seen her, he started to leave, then stopped abruptly. Slowly turning toward me, I noticed how hopeless he looked. His eyes were wide and watery, maybe even a little fearful, "You know I love her, right? If she'd go for it, I'd marry her today."

"Wow," I said as I processed his words. What would I give for Brock to feel that way about me? "I get it. Have you told her?"

He plopped on the couch and dropped his forehead to his hands. "Yeah. Every way I know how. She tells me she loves me too, but she isn't sure about commitment. I understand though." He looked up and stared at the wall. "Her parents are never around. No one has ever been there for her. You and Brock...well, you know. If she gave us a shot, we'd be great, but she won't. I'm not sure what to do."

"Whoa. Okay." I paused to collect my thoughts, but Neal was looking at me like I had all the answers. Didn't he know I was just as lost as everyone else? I couldn't figure out my own life, let alone Ivy's. "I don't completely understand what Brock and I have to do with anything, but Ivy has her own stuff." None of us even knew the extent of Ivy's "stuff," but she dropped plenty of hints when she was feeling dramatic or depressed. "We all do. You know I've been friends with her for ten years and never met her mom and dad? I know her brother but not her parents. She's had more new cars than anybody I've ever known. That huge house she grew up in was often empty. Ivy needs someone to love her, so don't doubt you're doing the right thing. All she needs is someone who's so in love with her that they never give up on her." That seemed like the right thing to say. I wasn't really one for giving advice, but telling someone to show a little love seemed like a slam-dunk.

I might have been wrong. When Neal said, "I hope you're right, Reagan. And maybe you should find a way to take your own advice," then stood and walked out, I questioned my ability to give even the simplest suggestion. It was the most bizarre encounter and left me feeling uneasy.

Hell or high water, though, remember?

Brock showed up at my apartment shortly after Neal left. His hair was wet from showering after the gym. Something about the wet hair, the jeans that hung from his hips, and fitted t-shirt made me lose my mind. The second he walked in the door I was on him. He caught me when I threw myself at him and lifted me so I could wrap my legs around his waist.

"Rea," he breathed.

"I need you," I told him.

He took my mouth. It wasn't just a kiss. He took control of my lips, my tongue, my body. Brock had this way about him. He could be so quiet but so commanding at the same time. When he was passionate about something, there was no stopping him. This time, it was me he wanted.

I was thankful it was dark because after we devoured each other, I found I was embarrassed by my rash behavior. Little did I know my actions was the beginning of the end.

Brock was lost in thought as well. His fingertips ran up and down my back as I lay across his chest. We were in my bed, but the door to my room was wide open. It wasn't like I gave him time to close it.

"What was that all about, Rea?" I sat up to move away, but he stopped me. When I looked into his brown eyes, I liked what I saw. There was sincerity there and maybe even a little love and adoration. He grabbed my hand to bring my attention back to the question. "Not that I'm complaining, but I know you. Something's up."

"Brock, I—" I froze. The words refused to come.

"What, babe?"

"I need to say something, but I need you to not interrupt me 'til I'm finished."

He leaned up on his elbows and raised his eyebrows. "Okay…"

"I've been thinking." I glanced up to my ceiling and let out a deep breath. I decided I couldn't stay lying across him like I was and moved away, covering my chest with the sheet. "That's not true. I've known this forever."

I felt sick to my stomach. How was it that I still didn't have the right words? How do you tell your best friend that everything you thought about love was wrong because he showed you what it could be like? How do you tell him that being friends with benefits wasn't enough anymore? I decided it didn't matter if what I said was perfect. I needed him to know how I felt.

"Brock, I'm—" The opening and slamming of my apartment door interrupted me.

"Reagan!" Neal yelled my name and repeated it

as he came closer to my open door. Brock sat up to cover me, but it was too late. Neal was standing at my door. By the look on his face, he wasn't registering the fact that I was naked. "Where is she?"

"Who?"

"Where is she?" He was out of control.

I flinched when his voice rose again, then pleaded, "I don't know what you're talking about."

Finally, Brock intervened, "Man, we've been here the whole time, and she hasn't been home."

"You guys don't fucking know! You have no clue!" he shouted at us.

Brock climbed out of bed and pulled on his jeans. He walked his friend to the living room, giving me a chance to throw on clothes. My phone started ringing right after I buttoned my pants. It was an unrecognized number, and a feeling of dread flooded my gut.

"Hello?" I answered.

"Is this Reagan Anders?"

"Yes."

"I think your roommate is here and in need of your assistance."

"Who is this?"

The bartender was calling from a seedy bar on the other side of town where Ivy had found two older men to buy her drinks. Then she took one into the bathroom leaving her phone and purse on the bar. She had apparently told the bartender to call me to come play. He was not amused.

I could hear Brock still trying to calm Neal and realized that I had to go alone. I would rather Brock go with me for protection or for help carrying Ivy, but Neal couldn't know. This whole thing would be ten million times worse if he got involved.

I stepped out in the hall and tried to wave Brock discreetly back to my room, but Neal flipped out. "Was that her? Where is she? Something's wrong. I know it!"

"Man, chill out."

"It wasn't her!" I screeched then Neal came toward me and pinned me to the wall.

In a moment of rage unlike anything I had ever seen, Brock took Neal and threw him off me. "Stay away from her!"

I didn't know what to do, but getting away from Neal was necessary. "I'm going to look for her," I told them. "You two stay here in case she shows back up."

Brock stopped me at the door. "You okay, Rea?" He was always asking me that.

"Yeah, I'm good. Don't let him break anything."

Brock dropped a kiss on my lips and whispered "Be careful," like he knew where I was headed.

Neal groaned. "Can you guys do that some other time when Ivy isn't missing?"

With one last glance at Brock's worried face, I raced to my car and drove to the other side of town. I wasn't exactly sure where the bar was, but I was familiar enough with the area to know where it could be. I found it with little trouble when I saw a red neon sign that simply read: *'Bar'*.

The gigantic bouncer eyed me strangely then said, "You here for the girl?"

"Yeah." I nodded.

He returned my nod, then held the door open for me. The place was smoky and reeked of sweat and beer. It was an unpleasant combination, and I couldn't figure out why Ivy would come here. Needless to say, she wasn't hard to pick out. She was dancing on the stage to some country song that did not match the rhythm of her dancing.

"Reagan!" she cheered, then jumped off the stage to tackle me in a hug. "My girl is here, everybody!"

I looked around the room at all the drunken bikers slumped over their beers. It was definitely time to leave. "Okay, let's go, Ivy. Neal's been looking for you."

"Boo! I don't want to go back to him. He's no fun." It was then I saw how unfocused her dilated eyes were. She wasn't just drunk. She was on something.

"Sure he is. Now, let's get your stuff."

"No!" In a ninja-like move she grabbed my keys and bolted out the door. I was forced to chase her, and I reached my car just as she climbed in the driver's seat of my mom's old Camry. I didn't think. I just climbed in the passenger seat and immediately tried to talk her out of driving.

She didn't listen. She started the car and whipped out of the parking lot. "You know what it's like, Reagan?"

"What what's like?"

"Flying," she said as she whipped around a curve, making me buckle my seatbelt and hold on to the oh-shit handle.

"No. Why don't you pull over, and I'll drive?"

She ignored me. "We're all going to die eventually. We came into the world alone, and we leave it alone. The people we love only leave us, so what's the point?" She spoke with remarkable clarity for someone higher than a 747 over the Pacific.

"I don't know, I…Please pull over," I begged again.

"You love Brock. He loves you, but you torture each other."

"Neal loves you."

"No. Neal thinks he loves me. He wants to rescue me. Silly boy." She sped up, and I knew we weren't going to make it through this ride. The only reason we were still on the road was because no one else was. I tried to sneak my phone out of my purse to call Brock or nine-one-one. I wasn't sure which, but the second she saw it, she flipped out.

"Who are you calling?" she snapped angrily.

"No one," I promised.

The rest of the ride was silent except for the screaming in my head. I remained white-knuckled as I gripped the oh-shit handle with one hand and held my seatbelt tight with the other. I knew that tonight was the night I would confess everything to Brock if I could just make it back to him safely.

Somehow we survived the drive back to the apartment. How she knew where we were I would never know. I didn't even know where we were most of the ride, let alone how she stayed on the road.

As soon as she was sort of parked, she leapt out of the car, leaving it running and the driver's side door wide open. "What a rush!" she squealed as she leapt into Neal's arms right when he and Brock made it to the bottom of the stairs.

I was moving much, much slower, trying to calm my racing heart and keep myself from falling apart. An adrenaline rush was one thing. Riding in the car with a drunk and most likely high Ivy was not a "rush" like she thought. It was a brush with death and definitely not something I wanted to experience again.

Brock's face mirrored how I was feeling. His stride was stiff and quick as he passed Neal and approached me as I rounded the car. "She drove?" he asked when he reached me.

I still couldn't speak, so I simply nodded as I tried to pass him to straighten my car into an actual parking space.

He pulled me back against him. "I got this. You go inside." I shook my head against his chest, and he seemed to understand how I was feeling. "It'll be okay." I gripped his shirt in my hands, willing myself not to cry. I hated criers, and even worse, I hated crying. Brock held me tighter and whispered, "Shh. I got you. You're safe. She's safe. I'm right here."

Once my heart returned to a normal pace, I felt utterly exhausted, but I didn't want to go inside without Brock. I didn't want to see Ivy if she was still on her rampage, and I didn't want to deal with her if she wasn't. I just wanted to go to sleep in Brock's arms and forget the whole night. It seemed Brock felt the same, because we bypassed my apartment and headed straight for his. We climbed into bed fully dressed and wrapped around each other, where we remained until the darkness was gone, and the morning light had replaced it.

# Chapter Thirteen

*Now*

I hadn't had that flashback in a long time. I thought I had forgotten what it was like in the car that night, but the dream was as vivid as the when it happened. Before I could calm my racing heart, the bile started to rise. I raced to the toilet to expel everything inside my stomach, then I sank to the floor and sobbed. I knew what was coming. The next one would be worse. The memories would take over, and I wasn't sure if I could handle it when the images returned unchecked in my dreams. There was only one person who could have triggered the memories. I had pushed him away; I had pushed everyone away. Now that he had discovered my hidden cloud in the sky, he had become the one person I couldn't wait to see, and for that I knew I would pay emotionally. The only thing I wasn't sure of was if the trade was worth it. He was the one person who had the potential to break me.

It was a long while before I could pull myself

together, and I was late opening the store. I missed Restaurant Guy stripping in the parking lot and the morning ladies walking their dogs on their coffee run. Sandra Hillman was waiting outside the store for me when I arrived. She was there to pick up the next novel in her series that released that day, and I rushed to let her in the door before she started ordering her own books online.

"Sorry to point out the obvious, dear, but you look like hell. The only thing worth losing sleep over is a good man, so please tell me it's a man that's making you so tired."

"No, ma'am. No man. Just a bad night."

"Oh honey, you have to find yourself a nice man. You know, my grandson is coming to visit next week. I can set you up if you'd like. He's a good-looking man, but I couldn't tell you about his bedroom skills. If it's anything like his dancing, you're better off looking elsewhere. Sweet boy, though."

"All right then, Mrs. Hillman. Thanks for the offer, but I'm okay."

"Let me know if you change your mind. I'll drop some pointers before he takes you out." I could only imagine.

"I'm sure he'd find that very helpful."

I finished ringing her up with no more talk of her grandson and sent her on her way. Thankfully, the weather was nice, so a lot of people were out exploring the boardwalk. It was the end of the season, so it was mainly the locals who had retired here, but they kept me busy. Old people were so opinionated and liked sharing their thoughts with anyone who would listen. I always found them interesting, especially when I was in desperate need of a distraction.

Somehow the day passed quickly. Meyer had come and gone. The customers stopped trickling in, and before I knew it, it was time to close. A handsome face appeared in the window just as I went to lock the door. His smile when he saw me was unforgettable. It stopped me in my tracks until he approached me the rest of the way.

He pulled the door open and strode to me so fluidly, like he was floating or skating. The second he was close enough, he took my face between his big hands and pressed his lips to mine. Without thinking, I surrendered to his kiss. In one single moment, all the fear, regret, and hate gave way to desire. He was still the only one I wanted like this. Never had any man made me feel so desired and so needy. Usually I was making grocery lists or thinking about the store when I kissed someone. Not with Brock. Not ever. I couldn't remember what they sold at a grocery store, let alone make a list when he took control of my lips.

He pulled away first, but my lips followed his like they had a mind of their own. When I opened my eyes, he was grinning down at me. "I thought about that all day," he whispered.

"Did you now?"

"Seems you didn't mind."

"Kissing you was never the problem."

"No. Kissing wasn't the problem." His hands drifted from my face to my neck then across my exposed clavicle. "Touching was never the problem."

"Mmm." I audibly hummed when his lips touched my neck. I had always fallen stupid when he worked his magic on me. "I don't remember what the problem was right now," I told him sounding breathy and a little desperate. Don't judge. It had been a long time, okay?

Just as his lips grazed my ear, he said, "Talking was the problem, so let's do some of that before we get too distracted by this." He pulled away, then added, "I don't want you to have another reason to disappear on me."

I frowned, remembering my dream the night before and the reasons why we were in this predicament. He was right, though. This is what we always did before. Wasn't that the very definition of insanity? Doing the same thing over and over expecting a different result? It was time to make the mature decision and stop running from the truth.

"Let's do this. What did you have in mind?"

"If Jordan and Meyer wouldn't miss you this evening, I'd like you to join me for dinner at my house."

"I don't know how they'd feel about it—you'd have to ask them—but I will be happy to join you for dinner if you promise to keep your hands to yourself. I don't know how much talking we'll do if we open that can of worms."

"I can behave if you can. If I remember correctly, your hands tend to wander as much as mine."

He remembered correctly, but I wasn't going to give him the satisfaction of telling him he was right.

Instead, I stepped away. "Let me close the store, then I'm all yours."

"Music to my ears, Rea."

I cashed out the register and prepared the deposit, then left some notes for tomorrow. Brock watched me as I tidied up and did my usual routine, trying not to delay or rush. I didn't want him to think I didn't want to talk, even though I would rather do almost anything other than have a conversation about the past. At the same time I didn't want to rush and make him think I was hopeful for more. Hope was long gone and had been for a while.

"Ready?" he asked once I had my purse and cardigan in hand.

"Yep. Let's go."

"Yes, ma'am." Brock held the door for me, then held my purse as I locked the door. What a gentleman.

"What are you feeding me? I was late for work and forgot to eat lunch."

"You forgot to eat?"

"Shut up. My friend Melanie usually brings me lunch a couple times a week, but I didn't get a chance to call her back."

"Seriously, you too busy to eat?"

"Oh, stop!"

"How do steak and potatoes sound?"

"You eat carbs?" I asked mimicking his tone.

He wrapped one of his big arms around my shoulders and hugged me to his chest, allowing me to confirm it was as rock-hard as suspected. "Very funny, little one."

I followed him to his house, which appeared to be a one-story bungalow from the front, but I had a feeling there was more than met the eye considering its location. I wasn't wrong either. On the opposite side of the house were floor to ceiling windows overlooking the river that ran parallel to the ocean. The sun was preparing to set and the whole scene was breathtaking.

"Like what you see?" Brock asked from behind me. I could feel him but our bodies weren't actually touching. My body was still attuned to his.

"It's amazing."

I remained standing right inside the door until he took my hand and guided me to the other side of the scarcely-furnished living room. "Yeah, the house needs some work, but that view was worth it." Brock led the way to a deck that I now noticed was on the second floor of the house. There must have been a basement beneath my feet that couldn't be seen from the front side. "Have a seat. I'll get some drinks and fire up the grill."

When he stepped back through the glass door, he was waving a bottle of champagne and carrying two glasses in his other hand. I immediately recognized the bottle. "Dom." He grinned. "I remember getting ignored a time or two for expensive champagne. I figure we could enjoy this and each other tonight."

I snorted at the implication that we would be doing anything beyond having mundane conversation and eating whatever he came up with. There were two things I knew about myself. The first was that I could eat almost anything. The other thing was the second this conversation became too serious or too personal, I would shut down. I was almost looking forward to that moment when I wouldn't have to worry about the next question or uncomfortable nugget that would come out of his mouth.

While he poured us champagne in actual flutes that were nicer than any single man should have, I told him briefly about my encounter with Sandra Hillman.

"She sounds like she knows what she's talking about."

"I'm sure she does. The woman has had more pool boys, gardeners, and handymen than the entire city of Los Angeles combined. Of course that's just a rumor, but the woman is nearing eighty and still oozes sex appeal."

He laughed. "That's an odd thing to say."

"It's an odd thing to see," I replied seriously.

Dinner was amazing. He served the steak and potatoes restaurant style and paired it with a red wine even though I could have guessed he was still a beer drinker. I wouldn't have any idea when he learned to cook. I would have missed all his failed attempts at grilling, but I reaped the benefits of his practice. Needless to say, the man could cook, and the whole evening was the very epitome of romance…unfortunately.

We talked for a bit about him buying his home, then fell into a comfortable silence. Later we moved inside, and he started a fire and poured more champagne. The silence stretched, but neither of us tried to fill it. Yes, we were supposed to be talking, but it felt good to just be. Not to mention I was so tired from not sleeping the night before. The wine probably wasn't in my best interest either. I hadn't realized I was falling asleep until I felt the couch fall from beneath me.

"Shh," Brock whispered. "I've got you. I'm right here." The words were familiar, and I felt safe for the moment, safe enough to fall asleep again.

Later, when my brain started to wake, it was light out again. I registered the comfort and warmth of my bed—but it couldn't have been my bed. It didn't smell like my bed. It was harder than my bed, and what was the weight holding me down?

My eyes flew open as I remembered where I was. A groan coming from behind me had me freezing, especially when Brock pressed his hardness against my rear. As much as I wanted to respond, I remained still while trying to determine what the best course of action was. Did I try to sneak out of the bed and bolt? Or did I stay and have the conversation with him that we were supposed to have last night? Only one thing was certain, I hadn't slept that well in years.

"You're thinking too loudly. I can hear you over here." The humor in his voice made the panic in my head dissipate immediately.

I laughed. "I never expected to be in this position again."

He pulled me tighter against him. "Me neither, but I wished for it." The panic quickly returned.

I shifted to roll over, and he opened his arms to let me but pulled me close as soon as I settled. The butterflies erupted in my belly and settled quickly into contentment. I both loved and hated the feeling.

120

I hated myself a little more for what I said next.

"You did?"

He grinned, making his sleepy face light up. "Yeah, Rea. I dreamt about it. Wished for it. Prayed for it. Hoped for it. Needed it. Longed for it. For you. When you left, I—" He paused and rolled onto his back, tucking his arm behind his head to stare at the ceiling. "Until I met Jordan, I thought about it all the time, why you left. I never could piece it all together. I knew it had to do with the accident, but I couldn't figure out why you left me. Your mom said you couldn't see me when everything was going on, so I waited. I waited and waited for you to come back. A year later, you still hadn't returned. Everyone had told me to give up on you, but I couldn't."

"What does that mean, Brock?"

He rolled back onto his side to face me, then gently swept a loose strand of hair behind my ear. "It means I never gave up. Not on you. Not on us. There was always supposed to be an us. You were always mine even if you wouldn't admit it when we were kids. As long as you've been fighting us, I've been loving you."

It was my turn to fall onto my back. His words sounded nice enough. Part of me had been waiting forever to hear him profess his love for me, but the memories that were suddenly present in my brain reminded me that not all was as it seemed. I had stopped trusting Brock long ago, and I wasn't sure that was something I could overcome.

I really needed to go home.

# Chapter Fourteen

## *Now*

I made up some excuse and left the second Brock would let me. He knew he had crossed a line, but it was my fault. I shouldn't have stayed at his house. I shouldn't have fallen asleep. I shouldn't have drunk the alcohol…yes, blame it on the alcohol.

It was already happening. I was becoming that foolish girl who let things slide because she wanted the guy. What was it about guys that made girls stupid?

"You know there's no rush for you to move out, right, Reagan?" Zoe asked me as she put the groceries away in the cabinets. It seemed she moved in while I was playing stupid at Brock's house. "I told Jordan that you didn't have to move at all."

"No…I get it. It's time."

"That's what he said. He worries about you, though."

"Yeah, I know. He's a good brother," I said as I stood to leave. "He loves you, Zoe. It's time for him to have his own life without his sister always around." I just wasn't sure what I was going to do in the meantime.

I called Melanie to come up to the store to discuss my housing dilemma. I didn't make enough for me to get my own place unless it was on the edge of town and inconvenient to everything. I had savings, but I sunk every dollar I had into creating the best last bookstore anyone had ever seen.

"I'd let you stay with me, but I'm afraid I'd want to kill you. I haven't lived with anyone since I moved out of my parent's house when I was eighteen. I don't even like having house guests."

"No, I need my own place, but thanks for thinking of me…sort of."

She winked. "Anytime."

"Seriously, what am I going to do?" I hesitated, biting my thumbnail that become just a nub over the last few days.

"You might have to actually start selling books for what they're worth instead of giving them away," she suggested helpfully.

"If I raise the prices, no one will buy them. Everyone has an e-reader now."

"I don't."

"Yes, but your idea of reading for fun consists of Forbes and The Wall Street Journal."

"You're right. Today I read an article—"

"Stop," I interrupted with a groan. "I don't want to hear it."

"And this is exactly why you can't afford an apartment. Your business sense is somewhere in the bottom of the ocean along with your dating life."

"Hey! I'll have you know I had a sleepover with a man last night."

Her face lit up at my foolish confession. "An adult sleepover? Tell me more."

"It was really nothing, but I spent the night with Brock."

"And?"

"And nothing. We were supposed to be talking, but it felt more like we were catching up or on a first date. We had some wine, and I fell asleep. Nothing scandalous happened."

"You know it would be all right if something 'scandalous' did happen."

"Ha," I scoffed. "No. It most certainly would not be all right."

"Oh, Reagan. You have to let go of whatever happened in the past. It's time to move on with life. It's time to find your happy."

"I am happy."

"Yeah," she responded with disbelief. I didn't really believe it either. I existed, and everyone in my life knew it.

Melanie was a perceptive girl, and she knew we were heading into shaky territory. Instead of pursuing the conversation further, she slapped her hands down on the counter and stood. "Well, I have a date with an accountant."

"A real date or a business meeting?"

"You know the answer to that."

She was right. I did know the answer to that. Melanie never mixed business with pleasure. The sheer fact the "date" was with an accountant told me he was not on her list of suitable possibilities.

She went for the bad boy type...more like Restaurant Guy. Hmm...maybe they should get together. Then she would be distracted while I figured out what to do about—

Never mind. I was so not going there. There was nothing to be done about anything. He who came from the past shall remain in the past, and that was that.

Melanie left for her lunch "date" and a promise to meet up with me for apartment hunting later, so I distracted myself with searching for a new home online. I had plenty of time considering a total of ten people came in after lunch. One of them mistook the store for a florist. I wasn't sure how, considering books were attractively piled in the windows as a display, but there you have it. Men looking to apologize are even less observant than normal.

By the time Meyer arrived, I had a list of rentals to go see, and I was more than ready to close my store that seemed to have somehow run its weekly traffic away.

"So," she began once she climbed up on her stool at the counter with her snack. "Daddy says you might be moving soon."

"Yes, but I will still see you all the time."

"Oh, I know."

"All right. Then what's this about?" Nothing was ever easy with Meyer. She was building up to something.

"Does this have something to do with New Guy showing up?" Yeah, she called him New Guy too. We were awesome role models.

"Absolutely not." She paused and waited for more explanation. I wasn't sure how much Jordan had told his hyper-aware-but-still-too-young-to-know-everything daughter. "It has everything to do with your dad and me. It's time for me to fly the nest, Grasshopper. It was bound to happen sometime."

"Yeah, I know, but then who will I watch movies with?"

"Uhh…me. How about you come with me to look at these places with Melanie and me, and we'll find the perfect place to watch girly movies. You in?"

"Only if you buy me ice cream…"

"As if that was even a question."

\*\*\*

Seven rentals later and with our stomachs were full of double chocolate chunk ice cream, I was personally considering telling Jordan he was stuck with me forever unless he wanted to pay for me to live somewhere nicer.

Everywhere I looked that seemed to be in my budget had some hidden catch. The first place appeared to be great in the pictures, but when we pulled up to the place, I knew the images had been lying. The building seemed like it was hardly standing. The next place was a house, and it would have been great if I wanted to live with a family of rodents. By the seventh fail, I was done, and Meyer looked like she was about to crawl out of her skin. We went to the ice cream shop and washed our hands thoroughly before we dove into enough chocolate ice cream to cover dinner, dessert, and tomorrow's breakfast.

Who was I kidding? I was still getting a cinnamon roll for breakfast the next morning.

The big surprise was yet to come, though. When we arrived home, I had a visitor. I should have known he'd show back up, but after not hearing from him all day, I let myself believe the drama was over. I didn't even allow myself to think about how disappointed that made me feel because then I would be admitting that I wanted to see him again. And for the record, I didn't want to see him again. Okay...yes, I did, but I didn't want to want to see him again.

"How'd the search go?" Jordan asked as we walked through the door. I felt Brock's eyes on me as I dropped my purse on the counter and grabbed a drink out of the fridge. I knew he was grinning when he realized I was ignoring him to avoid the whole awkward, "Why are you here?" business.

"Great," I told Jordan as I continued to pretend my heart wasn't pounding thanks to the proximity of a certain someone.

Meyer followed up with, "She's being sarcastic," as if the other adults in the room hadn't realized it.

I dove into the description of each place, making everyone laugh at my theatrics. I may have been overdoing it just a bit to appear unfazed, but damn, what was I supposed to do? I had no clue how to act around him because he had me so screwed up in the head, I couldn't find the path back to normal if it was the only one left.

"Why don't you get someone who knows more about this to help you search? Doesn't Melanie know this area really well?" Zoe asked.

"Yeah. She plans to help me but tells me my budget is too pathetic for her taste."

"Of course it is." Jordan rolled his eyes. "Go ask the real estate guy who has the office near the store. He'll help you. He loves you."

"Yeah, and he's the skeeziest man alive. No, thank you, but nice suggestion, brother."

"I'll introduce you to my real estate agent. Maybe she could help you." This was from Brock. I could only imagine what his real estate agent looked like, but I only needed one guess for her hair color. Like I would want to hire someone like that to help me.

Then I had a brain to mouth malfunction. "Is she blonde?" Everyone's eyes whipped toward me. It must have been my tone. I didn't mean for it to sound like it did even though I meant it exactly how it sounded.

"No. She's a brunette." Brock chuckled. He liked that I sounded jealous. That only annoyed me even more.

"No thanks. I can find my own place."

"Suit yourself, but you do realize she would do all the searching and negotiating for you, right?" Brock knew how to go for the jugular. He knew there was no way I would take whatever was offered rather than find something I really wanted.

"Fine, but you guys have no say in what I pick."

"Sure."

"Fine," Brock and Jordan said in succession as

they wore twin expressions of mock seriousness, which told me they were both big fat liars.

I was doomed to have them overshadow this process, so I gave in when Brock offered to drive me to go look at places a few days later. The real estate agent didn't waste any time when Brock called her. She set up appointments at several places, which I foolishly told the guys about. When Brock and Jordan held out their fists to play paper, rock, scissors for who got to go with me, I knew I was in trouble.

In the first round, Brock threw paper and Jordan threw scissors. "Best two out of three," Brock said, just in case the rules weren't clear.

The next time they both threw scissors. Then Brock beat Jordan's scissors with rock. It was one to one and the deciding round. Brock threw scissors and Jordan threw...yep. He threw paper. Brock raised his arms in victory then shouted, "Ha!" as he pointed in Jordan's face.

"And it's a good thing. I know real estate," he bragged before grabbing my arm and leading me out to the car.

And what he meant by "knowing" real estate was that no place was good enough. The afternoon went a little something like this:

"Absolutely not."

"Nope. We're not even stepping foot in that place."

"It looks nice from the outside, but do you really want to hear your neighbors going at it through these paper-thin walls?"

"Why did they bother calling these houses single

family units if they built them right on top of each other?"

"Uhh…no. Get back in the car, Reagan."

By the end of the day, I was defeated and tired. Brock wouldn't shut up about the lack of decent real estate after he was the one who insisted on the great finds his agent could locate for me. Finally, I turned to him and said, "Brock, shut up."

His mouth immediately closed, and his eyes widened.

"I'm sorry, but I get it. There isn't anywhere in this town I can live that meets your standards and my budget. No need to harp on it."

His free hand reached for my neck, where he started rubbing the knots out. "Sorry, babe. You know I just want the best for you."

"Yeah, yeah, yeah." I turned and watched the sand dunes pass us by. What the hell was I going to do? Jordan wanted me out. I knew my brother would let me stay as long as I needed, but just knowing he wanted me gone was enough to push me out the door…only I had nowhere to go.

"We'll find you the perfect place," Brock said as if he could read my thoughts.

"Hope so," I responded, trying to appear unfazed by the day. I didn't want Brock to take care of me. I didn't want to depend on him for anything, especially not emotional support. He was known to let me down.

"How about we grab some junk food and go back to my place and watch whatever reality TV show you want to watch? By the end of that, you'll feel better about your situation." He knew me too well. Reality TV stars were the train wreck I couldn't stop watching. They had always made me feel better about life because I was never as pathetic as they were.

Junk food and reality TV turned into joking and laughing and somehow cuddling. I wasn't quite sure how that happened, but I also didn't fight it. When my eyes grew heavy, I knew it was time to leave, but I felt warm and of all things, I felt happy. I couldn't force myself to go even though I knew it was trouble. I never expected the trouble to appear in my nightmares, though...not when I felt so safe there in his arms.

# Chapter Fifteen

## *March 2003*

"Library, then food. We can make it to the party if we go right after class," Ivy said, suddenly very eager to focus on school. It had been a few months since the bar incident, but I still wouldn't ride with her no matter how many times she swore she wasn't drinking or using anything.

"Sounds good. Although I don't know why you want to go to this party so badly. Are you hoping to catch Neal hitting on girls?"

"Something like that."

"You two are weird."

"Make up sex is the best. You should try it some time. It might bring the excitement back or get one of you to finally admit how you feel."

"Ha. Ha. You're hilarious," I told her with a solid dose of sarcasm.

"Why haven't you told him? Or at least had a conversation about what happened after graduation?" Ivy knew what happened at her party, mostly because she was witness to it all rather than me telling her. She poked and prodded until she had enough information to put two and two together.

"Because I'm not a whiney, needy girl. It's pathetic." Instead, I'll just secretly hope he'll one day come to his senses and tell me how much I mean to him, so I can simply say, "Me too." That's so much better.

She knew I wasn't telling her the whole story, I could feel it, but Ivy was smart enough to let it go. "Then maybe it's time you make him jealous. It's time to do something to make your relationship official."

"Sounds like a huge waste of energy," I told her, ignoring her stab at my relationship with Brock. We were kind of together, and that was enough for me for now. We were exclusive because there was no time for anyone else, and I didn't feel the need to worry about how I felt about him because it seemed he felt the same way even if neither of us ever said it.

"Like I said, try it sometime." Ivy laughed maniacally as she pushed through the doors to the library.

On the ride up to the fourth floor, where we now had a study room, I tried to quickly read over my assignment. Ivy was humming away like she just discovered an odd bacteria in a petri dish, which had me following her eyeline out the panoramic elevator.

Brock was sitting at a table in the library when he was supposed to be in class. It wasn't his presence that had me eyeing him with a feeling close to hate. It was the girl sitting next to him with whom I had a problem. I could only describe her as familiar and satanic. My hands gripped my assignment tightly.

"What is she doing here?" Ivy asked after noticing my reaction, or rather my lack of one.

"Didn't I tell you? UCLA didn't work out."

"Of course it didn't. She's an idiot."

"Mmhmm," I agreed as the elevator dinged, alerting us to the arrival onto our floor.

"So, what is she doing at the library with Brock?"

"Great question," I grumbled. Instinct told me to stay and watch from afar, but I followed dutifully along to work on my paper instead of staying in that elevator for the rest of the day stalking Brock and Candace like I really wanted to do. Feelings of inadequacy and uncertainty replaced all the good ones I had about mine and Brock's possible relationship. I was suddenly unhappy with our arrangement and wishing I had gone along with the profession of love that I had wanted to share with him for so long. At least then I'd know for sure.

"You gonna write anything?"

"What?" I turned to Ivy, who already had her books and laptop laid out on the table. My bag was still resting in my lap, and I hadn't even realized we were sitting in the room until she said something.

"Are you going to start working on your paper?" she asked slowly.

"Oh. Yeah." I tried to work on my paper, but my heart wasn't in it. I didn't feel up to writing about Thomas Hardy or Jane Austen or any other author for that matter. I wanted to know what Brock was up to with Candace.

When he came over later, I didn't ask, and he didn't tell me. In fact I would have never known anything was off if I hadn't seen what I did. I wanted him to tell me what happened. As soon as he came in, I asked, "How was your day?"

All he offered was a simple, "Good."

So, I asked, "What did you do?"

He responded as expected. "Worked on a project and went to the gym."

It was incredibly frustrating. Coming right out and asking him about her would have been too much for my foolish pride, so I pretended everything was fine. As usual, he saw right through me. He asked me a million times what was going on, but I could never bring myself to admit I was jealous.

Brock had a project due on Friday, so he was supposedly pulling an all-nighter in the lab on Thursday. I wasn't sure if I believed him or not. Trust me, I wanted to give him the benefit of the doubt, but there was this nagging voice inside my head that bothered me all night. I checked my phone over and over. No messages. No missed calls. I threw my highlighter down and gave up the pretense that I was studying. I sat on my bed, obsessing over Brock. He was the distraction on a night when I desperately needed a clear head.

My phone rang beside me, and I jumped, hoping it was Brock. Of course it wasn't. It was Ivy drunk dialing me.

"What's up, Ivy?" I answered glumly.

"Reagan! Can you come get me?" she cried. She sounded like she was sobbing and I could barely understand her, It took me a second to decipher that she called me for a ride.

"Yeah. Where are you?"

"Bar on Ninth Avenue," she wailed and finished with, "Hurry!"

I threw on some clothes and made it down to Ninth in record time. There were a few bars in that area, but I was looking for the seediest dump I could find. I knew that if she went to drink alone, it wouldn't be anywhere where we would have gone as a group. She wanted to be where nobody knew her name.

I saw the dump at the end of the string of respectable businesses and a brand new two-seater convertible parked right out front. I found her sitting on the curb in front of her car smoking a cigarette with black streaks of mascara under her eyes. She was violently shaking and staring blankly at the space in front of her.

I approached her as if she was a skittish kitten, or how I imagined I would approach one. Ivy never flinched, but she knew I was there. "Thanks for coming," she said with a gravelly voice. Had she been screaming?

"Always."

She scoffed at that. "Yeah."

"What's going on, Ivy? You don't smoke."

"No, cigarettes are disgusting." Surely you see my confusion here, but I knew better than to point out the obvious.

"Why don't we go back to the apartment? We

can eat ice cream and veg out. If you want to talk, I'll listen. If not, we can watch some stupid movie with a happy ending." I wanted to get back to the safety of the apartment as fast as I could. I was still waiting to hear from Brock, and I didn't have time for one of Ivy's tantrums that night.

"Yeah," she said, then stubbed out her cigarette. "Let's go."

I started to head to my car when she stopped me. "Let's take my car. I don't want one of these jackasses screwing with it. It's brand new."

It seemed odd that she cared about her car. Typically she hated the extravagant gestures from her parents, made in place of them actually being there. Every time she expressed her disappointment in her parents, they sent her a gift that cost more than our college tuition. I thought that might have been the reason she jumped down the rabbit hole this time, but it seemed I was mistaken. She also appeared to have sobered up a bit. Her speech was in no way impaired now, so I had no way of knowing just how bad off she was at this point in the night. She simply wanted to go home.

"Sure. Okay."

"You'll have to get the keys from Bartender Man. He won't give them to me." Yes, I thought that was both wise on his part and suspicious on her part, but I did what I was told. Bartender Man gave them to me without question and went about his business. It wasn't until we were on the two-lane highway that led to our apartment that I discovered exactly what I had gotten myself into.

The road was dark and just wet enough from the

rain that had come down on and off all day. The road had a hill on my side and a drop on the other. Trees parted only enough to fit the highway in between them. They were the perfect conditions for an accident, which was why I sped up when Ivy said, "I think about dying more than I think about living. I wonder what it would be like not to consciously feel anymore."

"It wouldn't be like anything," I told her as my foot pressed a little harder on the pedal in an effort to make it home faster.

"It would be freeing. That's what it would be." And then she stopped talking altogether. For a moment I thought she fell asleep, but her eyes were wide open. I searched my brain for something thoughtful to say, but I was never good in times of crisis.

It was silent. The radio wasn't even on, and the road felt like it was forever long. Like the light at the end of the tunnel, I saw the traffic light up ahead casting a green glow on the street. That intersection was the final turn to head back to the apartment. For some reason, I knew that light meant safety.

I was so focused on the destination that I didn't see her hand coming. We were less than a hundred feet from the intersection when Ivy leaned across the car and pulled the wheel, forcing the car to veer quickly off the road. Without thinking, my foot went for the break, but all too quickly we were off the embankment and flipping. One. Two. Three flips before the car slammed against the tree. I was buckled in tightly and trapped in the car. My window was against the wet ground, and I knew if I could find a way to unbuckle my seatbelt, I could climb through the non-existent windshield.

My mind wasn't working clearly, though. At no point while I struggled to free myself from the car did I notice that I was alone. Ivy was nowhere to be seen.

# Chapter Sixteen

## *Now*

"Reagan? Jesus, Rea, you're shaking. Reagan!" Brock's voice came through the darkness. I couldn't force my words out, though. The memories were always so vivid. Even after all this time, it was like I was still trapped in that car, realizing Ivy wasn't there. The physical scars faded, but the emotional damage would simply not disappear.

"Rea? Breathe, Reagan. Just breathe. I've got you. You're safe."

I opened my eyes to find Brock hovering over me. His face was so familiar, but there were differences as well. He didn't have so much facial hair before. There were small lines from years of making the same facial expressions. His eyes were the same, though. The dark lashes that women would kill for almost touched his eyebrows when his eyes were wide, like they were right then.

"Brock," I whispered.

He swiped his thumbs across my cheeks, and it

was then that I realized my eyes were leaking. I couldn't be crying because I wasn't a crier. Only weak people cried, and weak was the one thing I absolutely could not be.

I moved to sit up, causing us to bang our heads together. His hand flew to his nose while he groaned, and I cried out in pain. "Sorry!"

"What are you doing?"

I was crawling away, trying to get out of the mess of sheets that seemed to be caging me in. "I have to go. I need to go home."

"Oh, no you don't." He grabbed me from behind and pulled me back against his bare chest. "You aren't going anywhere until you tell me what that was." His words sounded harsh, but his tone was consoling. Brock cared about me, no doubt about that. However, my nightmares weren't something I wanted to share. Not with anyone.

"I can't, Brock. I can't talk about this."

"Reagan, you have to talk about that. You had a panic attack."

"I know."

"How often does that happen?"

"Never…not anymore."

"So, why now?" Then he paused, and I felt it the second he realized. "It's because of me, isn't it?"

"Please," I begged, "I can't do this."

"Reagan, I only want to help you. What can I do to fix this?"

"You can't. I can't.

"Why can't you, Rea? What if you knew talking would help you?"

"It won't!"

"How do you know?"

"Because I don't trust you!"

"Why not?"

"I was there. You weren't. I have to live with it. You don't. Now let it go. Let me go."

He didn't. If anything, he gripped me tighter. It was his silent way of telling me that he was seeing this through. He wasn't going to let me go no matter how far I ran. After everything…after all this time, Brock was still fiercely loyal, but he was done letting me have my way. Now, he was in charge, and there was no more hiding for me.

We remained like that for a long time. I was sure we both had other places to be, but he held me to him with the strength of a protector until I felt safe…until I had no other choice but say the words that I had never spoken out loud.

"I killed Ivy."

Silence stretched for too long. The air conditioner came on and shut off again. Brock's grip on me never waned.

Finally, I added, "They determined it wasn't my fault, but it was. That email meant nothing. I knew how dangerous she was. If I had gone with my gut, she would still be here. The judge might not have blamed me, but he should have. Her parents were right. Ivy's death was all my fault."

Brock's solid hold on me broke, and I thought he was going to let me go. Maybe I thought he was going to push me away. I wasn't sure, but I knew the second his arms loosened from my body, my heart tore in half. It was exactly as I suspected. No one wanted to know the truth.

But then his hands rested on my waist before lifting me and turning me around, as if I was no heavier than a child. My eyes remained down until he held my chin between his thumb and pointer finger. The second our eyes met, he said, "You listen to me, Reagan, and you listen hard. That's the biggest bunch of bullshit I've ever heard come out of anyone's mouth. Ivy wasn't in her right mind. She was using all kinds of drugs to find an escape. Do you think that was the first time she tried to off herself?"

No, I knew it wasn't.

I shook my head. "You weren't in the car with us, Brock. You don't know."

"Do you know how many times Neal had to stop her from doing something stupid? She told him once that she didn't want to die alone. Reagan, she tried to take you with her. None of that is on you. It was all planned. The new car. The dark road on the rainy night. She confessed everything to Neal long before it happened."

"You knew?"

"He put it all in his deposition. Did your lawyer not tell you?"

"You knew?"

"I tried to tell you. I called you. I came by your mom's house. She said you wouldn't see anyone."

"Because of this," I exploded.

"Because of what?"

"I was tired of the push and pull. I was tired of the girls. Then everything with Ivy happened, and no one told me anything. I knew in my gut that I couldn't trust you. You should have told me how

143

dangerous she was. I should have known."

"I didn't know until her funeral," he pleaded. "By then you weren't talking to me, and I had no idea why."

My mind was reeling, trying to place everything in order, trying to make sense of it all. "I saw an email, but I don't know. It didn't say who the email was to. I wasn't exactly in my right frame of mind by the time the Dunns filed charges against me. I've spent the last decade forgetting any of it occurred."

"Even me."

"Especially you."

"Why?" I could clearly hear the hurt in his voice, and another piece of me broke. Soon there would be nothing left.

The words sat there on the tip of my tongue. If he pushed, they'd fall out, and I didn't want to say why I pushed him away. I didn't want to tell the truth.

"Why, Rea?"

I bit my lip to keep quiet as the frustration built inside of me. He was always like this. He always pushed too hard. I used to avoid him when I had something to say and didn't want to say it, but new Brock wasn't letting this go.

"Tell me, Reagan."

"Because part of me blamed you for what happened."

"Me?" he asked incredulously.

"Well, not you exactly, but me."

"I don't understand."

"You were a distraction. I didn't trust you, and I certainly didn't trust myself when it came to you."

"What the hell does that mean?"

"If I hadn't been obsessing over you, I would have known better, paid better attention, seen the signs, reacted faster, but you were weighing on my mind because you were with Candace!" By the end of my rant, my voice was screeching at an all-time high decibel, and I was breathing heavily. Brock's arms remained tight around me, and I could feel us both trying to calm ourselves.

Finally, after a long moment, he broke the silence. "So, you left."

"So, I left," I confirmed. "My mother was worried about me, so eventually she sent me to my father. She thought if she could fix that one thing, I would be able to feel again."

"Did you learn to feel again?"

"Yes."

"What happened?"

"I met my brother."

# Chapter Seventeen

## *The Day After The Accident*

"She's dead, Reagan." I didn't look up from my mangled arm at the sound of that voice. It wasn't the voice I was so desperate to hear, nor did it offer any comfort or relief. "Did you hear me? You killed her. You killed Ivy."

I still didn't respond. Even knowing he was right, I couldn't look up from the evidence of the accident that should hurt so badly. Strangely enough, my broken and bleeding arm felt distant. I stared at the drying blood as if it wasn't my own, knowing that what Neal said was the truth. I killed Ivy. My friend was gone...no, not gone. Dead. My friend was dead. I killed my friend, my roommate. The words played over and over in my head as Neal continued to shout at me. I knew he wanted a reaction, but I couldn't give him that. I killed her, and all I could do was stare at my mangled arm wondering where it all went wrong.

"Sir, I'm going to have to ask you to leave," a

nurse said, catching my attention. She was the one who had gone to gather the materials to clean and wrap my arm after the x-ray. She seemed nice.

"Yeah, I'm going. I can't look at this heartless bitch anyway."

"Sir!" My eyes shot up to the door at the change in the nurse's tone. "That's enough. Please leave."

He did. He marched right out the door while the nurse gave him a stern look that would make Stone Cold Steve Austin avoid messing with her.

"Let's get you all fixed up now," she said to me in a far friendlier tone. I tried to smile, but I think a pained grimace was all I could muster.

As she put the finishing touches on my plaster cast that I would be getting replaced after meeting with the surgeon, the detectives came into the room. I could tell right away who they were. If the suits and crooked ties didn't give it away, the giant badges on their belts sure did.

"Reagan Anders?" the taller one with the receding hairline asked.

"Looks like you found her, Detective," the nurse responded dryly.

"Yes, no thanks to you." This was from the shorter one. He had dark hair and pale skin, reminding me of a vampire, not of the Brad Pitt variety, though.

The nurse angel shook her head. "You couldn't give the girl a little bit to get herself together, could you?"

"It's been three hours since the incident. It's time to talk," tall detective said as he approached the chair beside the bed. "Miss Anders, had you been drinking or under the influence of anything tonight?"

I shook my head no. My throat felt raw, and emotion was starting to bubble to the surface. I physically couldn't get words out to answer him.

"You sure you didn't have a couple of drinks? Smoke a little dope?" Vampire Detective challenged.

"I can answer that." This was from the doctor who was entering the room, carrying a chart, followed by my mother.

"Reagan!" she cried. "Dear heavens, are you all right? What happened?"

"Ma'am, are you her mother?"

"Yes, of course."

"We need to gather information from your daughter. You can remain in here as long as you don't interfere." Then tall detective turned to the doctor and prompted him to continue.

"Her labs show no foreign substances, that she's not pregnant, and with no history of seizures and no vision problems, she appears to have been in her right mind."

"Of course she was," my mom said, earning a glare from the vampire. "Oh, don't you look at me like that. If this were your child sitting here, you'd be doing the same thing. Can't you wait to speak with her once she's not in the emergency room?"

Tall Detective looked effectively chastised while Vampire Detective just looked...pale. "Yes, ma'am," Tall Detective responded. He handed my mother his card with instructions to meet him at the station.

My mother was a stickler for following the rules, so after I was squared away at the hospital and had my appointment set with a surgeon, she drove me to the police station. I still hadn't spoken to anyone. I still couldn't believe what happened. The scene played over and over in my mind. Ivy pulled the wheel and down the embankment we went. When was she thrown from the car? How did I end up with just a broken arm when she was…well, you know…she was dead?

The interview lasted forever. We sat in what looked like a conference room, not in one of those scary interview rooms. They asked question after question, and my responses were all similar. "I…" I would start, then stumble over my words before saying, "I can't remember."

Because I couldn't. Everything was all jumbled in my mind. I remember worrying about Brock, then leaving to pick up Ivy. Suddenly, everything after I reached the bar was a blur. I couldn't remember what she said. I couldn't remember how we ended up swerving off the road, and the harder I tried, the less clear it became.

Finally the vampire detective, otherwise known as "bad cop," slammed his fists down on the table. "Look, between the evidence at the scene, the message on your phone, and the report from the bartender who conveniently showed up in the hospital waiting room, we know this was no accident. We're also fairly certain that Ms. Dunn orchestrated the whole incident, but you're not giving us anything. How can we help you if you can't remember what happened?"

My eyes widened in shock. I never would have believed he was actually trying to help me, but it still didn't matter. I couldn't seem to remember what happened.

The tall cop, previously thought of as "good cop," slid my mother a business card. "Take her home to rest. Call us if she remembers anything. We'll be in touch." With that, both cops stood from their chairs, grabbed their papers, and left the room.

"Come on, sweetheart," my mom said gently as she wrapped a hand around my arm. "Let's get some clean clothes and head home."

I simply nodded and followed her lead out to the front of the building, where Neal appeared. My mom saw he wanted to speak to me and left us to bring the car around.

"They're letting you go?" he asked. His voice was no longer laced with malice. He sounded more exhausted than anything. I knew the feeling well.

"Yes," I replied plainly.

"No charges?"

I shrugged because I wasn't sure what was to come yet.

"I'm sorry about what I said earlier," he mumbled, surprising the hell out me.

"It's fine. Nothing I haven't thought myself," I confessed. Then I asked the one question that had been plaguing me all day. "Where's Brock?"

Neal snorted. "You don't even want to know."

"Why not?"

"Let's just say, he was too busy to know anything that happened last night. If he'd known, I assure you, he would have been there for you today." Neal started to turn away when my mom's car pulled around front, then paused. "Good luck to you, Reagan. I honestly think you're in for a world of shit, and I don't think there's any way around it at this point."

I wasn't sure exactly what he meant, but I knew he was right. I just didn't know it would come at me from all sides.

Within the hour we arrived at my apartment, where I expected my mom to help me shower, then pack a bag to head home with her. I didn't expect to never make it out of the car.

She parked, and we remained buckled into our seats as I stared at the door to the apartment that I shared only yesterday. She saw my hesitation to go back into that apartment that would smell of Ivy. "Everything will be okay, Reagan. We'll get this all sorted out."

I took in a shaky breath. "I don't know if there is anything to sort, Mom. What they were saying was true," I admitted carefully. "I just can't remember how it all happened, even though only hours have passed."

"You're exhausted and in shock, sweetheart. No one expects you to remember. It's their job to ask questions, though."

"Yeah," I responded blandly. I wasn't concerned one bit about the questions they would ask because the impact of last night hadn't fully sunk in yet. Part of me still believed Ivy would be passed out in our apartment. An even bigger part of me was still distracted with my obsession from the night before. My eyes traveled up the stairs on instinct, like a magnet pulling my attention to what fate had in store for me. The door to the third-floor apartment opened. I expected Brock to appear so much so that my stomach twisted thinking about his reaction to my bruises and injured arm.

It wasn't him though. Candace Wood stepped out with wet hair and shoes in her hand. As long as I live, I would never forget the way it felt to see her step out of his apartment after the night and morning I'd had.

It was only then that he appeared. He had on jeans and a wrinkled shirt, looking every bit as disheveled, but at least his hair wasn't also wet from what I could tell. It didn't matter. I had seen enough.

"Let's go, Reagan. Let's get you packed."

Ivy wasn't going to be in that apartment.

Brock really couldn't be trusted.

Everything that was normal yesterday seemed lost today.

My heart felt heavy. I would go as far as to say that it hurt.

"No, Mom. I can't go up there. Just take me home."

My mom opened her mouth to say something then closed it. I shared that apartment with Ivy. She wouldn't argue with me wanting to avoid it, but she also wasn't one to miss signs. She followed my eyes to the stairs where Brock was trailing Candace, both of them smiling about something.

"Yes, let's get you home," she said without any indication of what she was thinking. In that moment, my heart felt a lot like my arm. Broken with the possibility of irregular healing.

# Chapter Eighteen

## *May 2003*

The detectives were in touch as promised. They called when Ivy's parents arrived in town with their high-powered attorney to press charges against me for vehicular manslaughter. They stopped by the day of her funeral, for which I hid in the back of the funeral home until I couldn't take it anymore. It was seconds after they wheeled her closed casket to the front. It was white and covered in light pink roses. The minister said three words before I signaled to my mother that I couldn't stay.

"Ivy Dunn was—" That was all I could hear. I didn't want to hear what he thought she was, because at the end of the day, she was dead, and that was all she was. And it was all my fault.

When the detectives called a few days later to ask me again what I could remember, I still couldn't give them anything. Once the case was passed on to the district attorney, I had the pleasure of dealing with my own lawyer. Between the meetings with the attorney, the doctor's appointments, and the trauma counselor my mother insisted I see, I didn't have much time for anything else. But it didn't matter; I was too tired for more anyway.

Even in my depressed state, I still thought about Brock, not that I ever voiced that to anyone. I was either wondering where everything went wrong with him or constantly predicting the impending doom I was going to soon face. It was a toss-up which of the two was worse: jail or a padded room for when I went completely crazy. I couldn't decide which I preferred. At least in jail, I'd have everyone else's drama to distract me.

The detectives came by on a Tuesday to let us know the charges had been dropped. They explained that someone came in and gave a deposition that had them investigating Ivy further. They found her emails, one in particular, that essentially cleared me of any responsibility. When they showed it to me, I couldn't believe it. The highlighted part read:

Don't worry. God won't let me die. I stopped wearing my seatbelt years ago. With as many red lights as I run, you'd think a truck would have already hit and killed me, but no. Do you know what I have ingested in my body over the last several months? I must be superhuman because I'm still here. One day I'm going to really tempt fate, and God won't know what to do with me.

Sometimes I think that if I just drive over a bridge and whip my steering wheel to the right, I could go over the side and crash to my death. God would probably laugh at me and say, "Not this time, Ivy." Maybe it would be easier if someone else was driving. Then I could take a friend with me to hell. God wouldn't give in that easily, though, would he? I think God likes a challenge, and this game we're playing is dangerous. I'm just not sure for who anymore.

I read the words, and yet it didn't sink in. I was still grieving my friend. Surely she hadn't planned my death along with hers. Did Neal know about this? I couldn't see who the email was to, but if he had known, surely he would have told Brock, and Brock would have warned me. Did Brock know and not tell me? Suddenly my decision to stay away from him made complete sense. It was an instinct I had that day I saw him and Candace together, but maybe my gut had been telling me more.

My mom thought speaking with the detectives would ease me out of my depression, but I slipped further and further into a dark hole instead.

*I killed my friend.*
*I killed Ivy.*
*Ivy planned it.*
*Ivy tried to kill me.*

*Ivy is dead.*

The thoughts were on repeat daily. When I slept, I dreamt of the accident. I had visions of Ivy pulling the wheel, so eventually I stopped sleeping. When I was awake, the only thing I could do was let the thoughts play. My brain flipped from remembering Ivy to wondering about Brock. It was a vicious cycle from which I couldn't escape.

Finally, my mom thought I needed to get away. I honestly think she was sick of me or didn't know what to do with me anymore. By Friday, she had me in the car on the way to my father's house. I didn't question any of it. She was worried. It all seemed to make sense at the time. Everything seemed so out of reach for me.

"You're going to see your father. He knows you're coming," she had said. "You need to take a break from home. It just reminds you of Ivy and Brock." She knew I hadn't spoken to Brock since the accident. I hadn't spoken to anyone.

My thoughts were too chaotic to stay focused on one thing anyway, but when my mother suggested I go see my father, I wondered if he would be happy to see me. We spoke on the phone once since the accident. He was kind and supportive. He acted like a dad would, but I couldn't even fully appreciate it until my mother mentioned the visit. I became fixated on the idea that my daddy could distract me from the pain I should be feeling. Repairing our relationship would be just the thing I needed, so I finally agreed.

My mom helped me pack and loaded up a basket of healthy snacks that remained in the backseat in favor of the junk food I bought at the gas station on the way out of town. She drove me there and only made me call when we were five minutes away. Oddly enough, he sounded excited to see me. I felt…nothing.

As soon as I pulled up to the brick ranch, he stepped out the front door. He looked like my dad but older. I remained in the car for a second while I stared at him. He was doing the same to me from the front door. It was only then I wondered if this had been a good idea. Too late now, I told myself. I was already here. He had seen me, so it would be ridiculous if I bolted now. Besides, I had always been curious to meet whoever he left us for.

"Go ahead, Reagan. Everything will be fine," my mother said, but I noticed she wasn't getting out of the car.

He stepped off the porch and started down the walkway to my car. I let out a deep breath and opened my door. "Reagan," he said as he came closer. He gave me a warm hug that left me feeling, you guessed it, nothing. I should have felt warm or relieved, but his tense body didn't welcome me like most dads hugging their children. There was a reluctance there that made every interaction strained.

"Hi, Dad."

"Hi, Reagan," he responded blandly, as if I saw him every day.

"Thanks for letting me come see you."

"Of course. You know you're welcome here any time." No, I didn't, but okay. "Can I help you with your bags?"

"I just have the one." He followed me and pulled my duffel bag out of the trunk of my mom's car. He waved to her, and she barely waved back. She didn't even really say goodbye to me, but I understood. She knew I wouldn't react anyway. What was the point of saying goodbye to someone who wasn't really present?

There was an awkward moment of silence before he nodded toward the house. He led me down the path into the house. The rose bushes outside were fragrant, and the floral scent followed us into the house.

"Your room is over here." We walked through the large family room with a floral sofa set and traditional furnishings from the nineties. It was so unlike the dad I used to know that I assumed his wife must have decorated without his input. Down a hallway, he showed me a bathroom and then the bedroom, which looked like a garden threw up in there. There was even a brass bowl of potpourri. I didn't even know they still made that crap. It explains why the house smelled like an old lady, though.

Dad dropped my bag on the bed. "Do you want to get settled or would you like me to show you around?" He seemed anxious, almost like he was hoping for something, but I wasn't sure which response he wanted.

I took a shot. "Show me around."

I must have picked the wrong answer because his face looked physically pained. I didn't change my mind despite his expression. I wanted to know why he was being so weird.

159

"Clara is at the grocery store," he said as he slowly moved down the hall. "She wants us all to have dinner tonight. She's made lasagna but wanted to include a salad in case you were worried about healthy eating like your mom."

"I'm not."

"I figured." He shrugged. "This is the living room." He kept walking, so I kept following. "Kitchen," he said when we entered the large space with wooden cabinets and laminate countertops that probably came with the house. The appliances were white, and everything was perfectly clean. I smelled something cooking instead of the overwhelming floral scent. I missed the smell of fresh linens at my mom's house, but I was trying to forget. It would be easy to forget everything. Everything felt so foreign that my mind kept taking in new things.

"You hungry or thirsty?"

"No." I shook my head.

"Okay." He guided me through the dining room, then pointed to another hall. "My bedroom is down there. My office is over here. Another bathroom…" And we were back in the living room. Why was this so awkward?

I looked around to avoid looking at him, expecting something more than what he was willing to give when my eyes caught the pictures on the mantle. They were family portraits. A man—my dad—a woman who I assumed to be Clara, and a boy that grew into a teenager. There was another picture of the boy at a graduation, then another at the beach. Who was he?

"He's your brother." My dad answered my

unspoken question.

"I have a brother?"

"Yes."

Suddenly I was feeling again, and it was anything but a good feeling. My insides felt like they were going to explode out of me with everything coursing through my body. I had a brother! I had a freaking brother! All the nothingness was gone and replaced by anger. My breathing became shallow as I fought against the scream tearing at my throat. I always thought I was a fairly rational person, but right then my mind was out of control. My heart pounded, and my cheeks flushed as the heat inside me bubbled up.

"What!" tore out of my body. It felt alien, like it wasn't even me screaming.

"He's your brother. I knew Clara before I married your mother. You knew that."

"But I didn't know I had a brother."

"I don't know what to say to you. I failed with you. They were my second chance," he pleaded.

"You didn't fail with me until this moment. How could you, Dad?"

"Don't put all the blame on me. This is the first time you ever came to visit."

"That's no excuse!" I screamed. "I was a kid when you left." My tone had not settled. The calm had not come, and I feared I would forever be shaken by this moment. "You kept a brother from me!"

Silence stretched between us until the sound of a garage door polluted the tense air. Dad's eyes widened slightly before he said, "What's done is done. It's time for you to quiet down. Why don't you get settled in your room while I help Clara with the groceries?"

In utter disbelief, I stormed away and hid in the hideously decorated guest room while they spoke quietly in the kitchen. I paced the length of the room while trying to process everything once again. I had a brother. A brother. My whole life I had believed I was an only child. I was raised as an only child. My mother hadn't so much as dated a man with kids, and suddenly I found out I have a brother. I considered if I wanted to know about him, to know him. How old was he? Where was he? Would I meet him? I had so many questions, but I knew I needed to calm down before I spoke to my father again. Another outburst would get me nowhere with him. My father used to walk away when I cried as a baby, not to mention the infamous Magic Kingdom experience.

A knock on the door startled me, but I figured it was my father coming to talk. I opened it to reveal a petite, dark-haired woman instead. Clara was beautiful and timeless. Despite her decorating, she was simple in her appearance. Her straight hair fell to her shoulders, and if I didn't know my father had met her in high school, it would have been hard to determine her age.

"Reagan?" She greeted me without a smile. "I'm Clara. Your father told me how things went earlier. I thought I should check on you. He's so bad in delicate situations."

You could say that again.

"It's fine. I'm fine. It was just a surprise."

"I can imagine. Why don't we have dinner, and I'll tell you anything you want to know?" Of course, Clara had to be super nice. I couldn't even hate her for taking my dad if she was going to be like this. I had planned my whole life to hate this woman, and my dad had to go and distract me with the news of a sibling, something I longed for my whole life. Now I was too busy hating my dad to think twice about Clara.

I asked question after question at dinner. There was no talking unless I was imposing or Clara was responding. The food was fine, but I don't even really remember it. I only ate to have something to do while I thought of what to say next.

While my dad cleared the dishes and started loading the dishwasher, Clara turned to me. "I'm glad you and your father are spending time together. I think you both probably needed to spend some time face-to-face, but if you being here is too much for him, I'll have to ask you to leave. I won't have my family destroyed because of your hurt feelings."

Sure, I was taken back by her candor, but at least I knew where I stood with her.

\*\*\*

I spent a week at my father's home before I finally asked to meet my brother. Jordan was his name, and he was three years older than me. In the time I was there, I had wanted to call Brock no less than a million times. He had once been my best friend and confidant, but every time I picked up the phone I saw Candace walking out of his apartment, the one above the place I once shared with Ivy. The thought reminded me of the way Neal blamed me for her death. By the time I thought of Ivy lying in that mahogany casket, the numb feeling had crept back in and completely taken over again. The cycle was predictable, and I was teetering on the edge of insanity.

For the first few days, I drove around the town to distract myself. There was a cool deli in the downtown area that I liked. I would sit in their booths and read in the afternoons while I tasted their menu. For them my taste buds returned, but either Clara was the blandest cook in the world or the discomfort I felt around my father would cause my senses to disappear again.

The "family" dinner was scheduled for a Sunday. My father spent the day working in the yard. Clara ran errands, and I holed up in the guestroom and read a book. I was trying to keep my nerves under control without starting the whole Brock-then-Ivy-then-blackout cycle. It wasn't working.

The truth was I missed Brock. I missed talking to him. I missed him holding me. I missed everything about him. He was supposed to be the one to make me feel better, but thinking of him only made things worse. I knew he had called. I knew he stopped by. My mother sent him away each time. Finally she stopped answering the phone when she saw he called because she knew what my answer would be. I couldn't allow myself to fall back in that trap, no matter how much I wanted his comfort. Now, I was far enough away that he wouldn't show up. I was hoping this would be the beginning of a fresh start.

I heard the front door open and close. A deep voice called out, "Mom? Dad?" I cringed knowing someone else was calling him dad. My stomach rolled, and a newfound hate for my father gutted me. How could he keep this from me for so long?

I didn't have time to lose it, though. I had to put my big girl panties on and meet my brother. It wasn't his fault our parents sucked. He was just an innocent bystander. Or was he? Did he know about me? Was he the reason we never met? Did he not want to meet me?

These thoughts had me flipping out all over again. What if he was the reason my dad never came around anymore? The questions churned in my head as I dressed. This was worse than going on a blind date—not that I really knew about that, but I could imagine. At least on a blind date, there's the chance you would never have to see each other again, and it wouldn't matter. If I never saw my brother again after this meeting, it would be almost as disappointing as missing the first twenty years. Maybe it would be more disappointing. I wasn't sure. Right then, I wasn't sure about anything.

From the pictures, I had an inkling of what to expect, but seeing him in person was different. He was taller than my dad but looked similar to him. His behavior wasn't far off, though. Jordan barely acknowledged me before sitting down and shoveling food on his plate. His mother frowned at his manners but said nothing. My father didn't notice from what I could tell. He was too busy staring down, pushing his peas around with his fork.

Clara tried to carry the conversation for all of us.

She told me all about Jordan's many accomplishments like a good mother would. He rolled his eyes and shook his head at one point, but never contributed. I ooh'd and ahh'd to the best of my ability, which really meant I nodded my head and pretended my mouth was full.

Suddenly my father threw down his fork, making us all jump when it clanged loudly against his plate. "I'm sorry. I can't do this." He darted from the table, knocking his chair over in the process.

The three of us sat there stunned for a moment before Jordan shrugged and went back to eating. Clara sighed and massaged her temples. "Reagan," she finally said. "I'm sorry, but it's time for you to leave. You being here is too much. I wish things could be different, but your father is under a lot of stress right now. He can't handle anything else on his plate."

I couldn't even fault her for kicking me out. I wasn't her priority. It never mattered how she felt about me because she would never know me. I represented my father's lies and betrayal of my family for her, nothing more. I would have hated me as well.

I quietly stood and collected what was left of my dinner, which I left in the sink before heading to the guest room to pack. I never really unpacked, so it didn't take long. My father had left, and Clara disappeared into her bedroom. I didn't know where Jordan went, but I was leaving the house as if I had been there alone the entire time.

With my bag in hand, I left the way I came in, through the front door. I was surprised to find

Jordan sitting on the front step waiting for me. "I know you don't know me, but I figured you'd need a place to stay. It would be nice to actually have a conversation with my sister."

I let out a short, uncomfortable laugh. "Sister…"

"Yeah, it felt weird coming out of my mouth too."

I thought for a moment. It would be nice to get to know him, even if it was only for one night. "You wouldn't mind if I stayed with you? I'll leave in the morning."

He shrugged. "You don't have to. My apartment has two bedrooms."

And so it began…

# Chapter Nineteen

### *October 2003*

The first time I held Meyer was two days after she was born. For an entire two days, I paced the lobby of the maternity wing and napped on a hard sofa when I couldn't stay awake any longer. I was waiting to meet my niece.

It had only been a few months, but Jordan felt like he belonged in my world. We got along like a brother and sister who had grown up together, except for one glaring difference—we knew almost nothing about each other. It was fun getting to know him, but hearing what it was like growing up with my father wasn't always easy. The man he called Dad was leaps and bounds away from the man I once knew, but talking to Jordan was like a kind of therapy I never knew existed...much like Jordan, the brother I never knew existed.

So, when Jordan found out he was having a kid with a woman who didn't want children, it only made sense that I stick around to be an aunt. No one could have predicted how holding her would make me feel, though.

Her mother signed over her rights as soon as the nurse would let her. She checked out not five minutes after the doctor signed her release. She was lost in the wind, but Jordan didn't mind. Meyer was his from the moment she took her first breath. He also had me there to help him. The second the squishy little bundle was passed into my arms, I knew she was one of us. She was pink and wrinkly and oh so tiny. Who knew I could love someone so much?

I fully blame her little adorable self for what happened next.

Feeling the love, my guard was completely down. I had no defenses with all the rainbows and sunshine floating through the new-baby air. I wasn't even annoyed when my father and Clara showed up at the hospital. I smiled up at him as he gazed down at the sleeping baby in my arms. I imagined it was very much how he looked at me when I was born, how he might look at my daughter if I ever had one. It felt like a breakthrough moment for us.

The five of us welcomed her home like the odd family unit we had become that day. We tiptoed around each other as she slept and cooed like crazy people when she opened her eyes. My dad and Clara came back every day for the next two weeks, and our world revolved around the little angel that stole our hearts.

It was on the tenth day that I tried to speak with my father. I asked him, "Was this what it was like when I was born?"

He leaned his head back and smiled. "No, Reagan, you weren't a quiet baby. You wanted to see everything from the moment you arrived. The only time you would sleep was if I was holding you. Your mother couldn't get you to rest no matter what she did."

"Sounds about right."

"Even as a toddler, you always wanted me."

Some things never change, I thought unkindly, but ignored it in favor of listening to him tell me more about when I was younger.

"We would go to the zoo, and you refused to stay in your stroller. Finally I started telling your mother not to bother with it, and I carried you on my shoulders everywhere."

I wanted to ask what happened. Why did he leave? But, I knew it would kill the moment. It didn't matter. Jordan walked in the room, and my father's whole attitude quickly changed.

"Jordan was the opposite. I wasn't there when he was born. He didn't need me...still doesn't." He paused, and I kept my eyes on him as he watched Jordan across the room. "In a way I needed him, though."

Was he...no, he couldn't be trying to say...no...surely not.

"It was a challenge to get him to accept me. At first he paid no attention to the man in his house. He refused to call me Daddy. To be honest, he would hardly speak to me. I tried buying him gifts, taking him to every place that was recommended for kids, but nothing worked. Then I bought a computer. I planned to work from home, but Jordan was

170

fascinated by it. We bonded over Pong."

I couldn't hold back any longer. "You left because I was too needy?" I asked incredulously.

"It wasn't the only reason. I also wanted time with my son. And I loved his mother. I cared about your mother, but she wasn't Clara. And you weren't Jordan."

Okay, that hurts. I didn't know what to say after that. He was basically confirming what I believed my whole life. I wasn't good enough for him. If I had been different, he would have stayed. Then something else occurred to me.

"Why didn't you introduce us sooner?"

"Who? You and Jordan?" I nodded. "Because it was two different lives for me. One where I crumbled under the weight of expectations and the other where I worked hard to be a part of it."

"That's bullshit, and you know it," I whispered.

He turned to me, surprised by my serious tone. The puppies and flowers atmosphere could compromise my defenses but not my bullshit meter. It was still working just fine.

"Why, Dad?"

I watched as he deflated under the weight of the truth. "Because I didn't want you to meet. I was happy here, and I didn't want you to ruin it."

"What did you expect? That I'd never find out?" I was still speaking quietly, but my tone had gone from stern to downright angry.

"Pretty much. I hoped you'd stop needing me eventually. You had your mom, and she was a better parent than I could ever be."

"Do you know how selfish you sound?"

171

"I won't apologize for a decision I made a long time ago. It doesn't matter now, anyway. Look how close you and Jordan have become."

"No thanks to you."

"Reagan, stop acting like a petulant child. You never needed me. You only thought you did. Me leaving made you into a stronger person."

I stood, and this time I didn't whisper. I wanted him to hear me loud and clear. "This is literally the dumbest conversation I have ever had. You can tell yourself whatever you want, but you are the most self-absorbed, idiotic person on the planet if you think leaving me was the best thing for me. You choose to be the giant disappointment that you are. Don't make excuses when there aren't any to justify your behavior."

"Reagan, calm down. Don't be so dramatic," he scolded as quietly as he could.

"No, Dad," Jordan interjected. "She's right."

"Jordan, don't stick your nose where it doesn't belong. You'll understand now that you have a daughter."

"No, I won't, because I could never leave my daughter the way you left Reagan."

My father turned and headed to the door. "You're more like me than you think, son. Come on, Clara. We're leaving." Jordan simply shook his head and turned back to his baby girl, who was cooing in his arms as our father left.

I watched Jordan for only a second before it fully sunk in that he was truly nothing like our father. In a moment of pure class, I ran out of the apartment and down the stairs where my father was just getting to his car. "Hey Dad," I shouted. When his eyes were on me, I threw up both of my middle fingers and yelled, "Fuck off!"

# Chapter Twenty

### *Now*

Brock and I continued to lie in his bed and talk for the rest of the morning. It was like he opened up the floodgates and out poured years of misspent time. I told him more about Jordan and Meyer, and he expressed how happy he was that meeting Jordan was the thing to bring me out of my funk. We talked about Neal, who moved away and married a "nice girl." I still couldn't believe Neal was a large part of the reason the charges against me were dropped. I had always wondered about the charges suddenly going away but never asked my mom. She had been through enough with me.

"I always thought Neal hated me," I confessed.

"Nah, he hated the way we were together, or not together, depending on how you looked at it."

"Huh."

"He may have been a little jealous. He had a crush on Ivy since she came to our school in seventh. Did I ever tell you how he and I became friends?"

"You got in a fight or something in the gym?"

Brock laughed. "Yeah…over Ivy. He wanted her, and she always flirted with me."

"Did she?"

"Oh yeah. Remember, that was the year we had sex ed with Coach Temple. He taught us all about the birds and the bees. She offered to show me what it was all about right in front of Neal."

"What? In seventh grade?"

"Uhh…yeah. She started early."

"No. Her first was David Chandler in tenth grade."

"No. Her first was David Chandler in seventh grade at Mikey Washington's pool party. Neal was so jealous."

"Huh. Who knew? I used to ignore Neal because he was such a jerk to everyone. I never understood why you guys were friends, but I figured it was a guy thing."

"It was. Keep your enemies close. He was actually a cool guy once I spent time with him. But he really cared about Ivy once he took the time to really know her. He wanted to save her."

"I know." This time the mood changed at the mention of Ivy. A solemn vibe settled over the conversation, and I searched my brain for something to bring back the light mood we had been in moments ago.

"I really hated Candace Wood." Yes, that was the first thing that popped into my mind.

"I'm aware," he answered dryly. "I think everyone knew you hated her."

"Really? I thought I did a pretty good job hiding it."

"Uhh…no. Every time she walked in a room, you walked out. I'm pretty sure she flirted with me just to piss you off."

And all of the sudden I was annoyed as if it was still going on. "Seriously?"

"Yeah. She used to show up at my apartment all the time and ask if you were there. Then she'd want to study. I'm pretty sure she stalked me to get into my classes just to bug you."

"What the hell?" Then I remembered the day after the accident. Coming home to the apartment only to find her there. "The day after the accident—she was at your place."

"Was she?"

"Yes." I could see the image of her with wet hair carrying her shoes as if it was yesterday. "She was leaving and looked like she had just showered. You followed her out."

"Why didn't you say anything?"

"I was doped up on pain pills and only there to get my stuff before my mom took me home."

"And you didn't say goodbye?"

"We didn't stay. I couldn't go in that place. Not after everything. And besides, like I said before, I felt like if I hadn't been so preoccupied with my feelings for you, I would have been able to prevent the accident. Even that day, I was torn up about Ivy, but you were still the first thing on my mind. The way I felt about you…it wasn't healthy."

"Reagan." He sighed and dropped his head back.

"I swore to myself that I'd never let anyone

consume me like you did, so I stayed away. After the first year, it became easier to pretend you didn't exist. Then there was a point where pretending you didn't exist turned into a fear of seeing you again. I was afraid that if I saw you, I wouldn't be able to resist. After all that time, what would have been the point?"

And there it was. The truth of all truths.

\*\*\*

The conversation died after my last confession. Brock continued to hold me, but he seemed contemplative, and I had nothing left to say. His hold no longer seemed safe and comforting. I needed his words, his reassurance for that, but he gave me nothing.

Finally, I made my excuses and left. I needed to shower and change my clothes before getting to the store to open, late as it was. Damien and Kira would be stopping by, and I never liked to miss a book talk with them...even if my mind wasn't in it.

Like always, our book talk ran way over, and I found myself relaxing with each passing minute. These two were drama free. I didn't even realize it was closing time until Brock showed up. "Who is that?" Kira sang as she eyed Brock in his work clothes. I had to admit, he looked good dressed like that, but of course I had to wonder why he'd show up after the way we left things. My nerves, which had just calmed, jumped back into their hyped-up state at the very sight of him.

"He's a friend from high school." We may have

gotten personal with our reading choices, but that didn't mean they needed to know all of my business.

"Mmhmm," Damien teased.

"No. Not like that at all," I warned him, even though it was exactly like what he was implying.

"What's wrong with that? I think rekindling with a high school sweetheart sounds romantic," Kira cooed.

"This little Rea of sunshine doesn't like that term," Brock explained as he approached, obviously overhearing our conversation. Great. Just what I needed. "She thinks high school sweethearts are lame and doomed to fail."

"Is that true, Reagan?" Kira now looked genuinely concerned for me and Brock if that was the case.

"No. Not anymore. You and Damien are going to live a long and happy life together."

Kira looked relieved at my assessment and gave Damien a blinding smile. He returned her look of adoration with equal fervor, while I glared at Brock with enough disdain to make him laugh. They left on their little cloud of bliss, so I turned my back to Brock to ignore him and his sexy grin.

He loved throwing me under the bus, and I hated him for it right up until he wrapped his arms around me and whispered, "I'm sorry for this morning."

"You have nothing to be sorry for," I told him, even though I had desperately needed him to acknowledge the awkward tension that had developed between us.

"I do. I asked you to tell me the truth but shut

down when you told it to me. It's hard to think that all of this could have been avoided had I simply known what was going on. I would have pushed the girl away had I realized, but I thought you knew how I felt about you. I thought you knew you were the only girl in the world for me."

My breath was stuck in my throat. These were the words I had needed to hear back then. I couldn't have ever imagined feeling like this once he finally said them, though. My heart had never felt such a sense of fulfillment. It was like getting everything I never knew I wanted all in one breath.

"I don't know what she was doing at my apartment, but I spent the whole night calling you. Neal said something happened to Ivy. I never imagined you were involved. You know I would have been there. I was furious with Neal for not telling me."

"Why didn't he?"

"I have no idea, but I suspect it had something to do with Candace. You'd have to ask him."

"Not going to happen."

"It doesn't matter anymore. What matters is that I still feel about you now the way I did back then. You're it for me, and I don't want to make the mistake of leaving you wondering ever again."

"Oh?" I replied dumbly.

"Yeah, oh," he whispered just before his lips took mine. My body immediately molded to his in the familiar way that only two people who belonged together could. His hands dove in my hair and tugged to angle my head for a deeper kiss, and I didn't refuse. A girl could get used to that kind of enthusiasm.

When he broke the kiss, he kept his forehead resting on mine. "How about I take you to dinner, then back to my place?"

"More talking?" I was sure my disappointment rang loud and clear in the tone of my voice. I was still breathing heavily. The last thing I wanted to do right then was talk.

"Not if I can help it." That simple statement held more promise than everything else we'd said in the past twenty-four hours combined. And I craved the intention behind that promise more than I could describe. Ten years, people! It had been a decade since I had been with him.

We didn't make it to dinner. We hardly made it to the car. Heat poured from our eyes. Desire was evident in every touch. This was going to be a night to remember.

He opened the door for me, but his muscular body quickly trapped me against the car as his lips descended on mine. Our lips opened, allowing the spark that was brewing beneath to fully light. We were in for an explosion of epic proportions if this continued. One of us was going to have to slow things down. Then his hands lowered and gripped my rear like he was holding on for dear life, and I knew, I just knew there was no slowing this train down.

He ripped his lips from mine, breathing heavily, and he gently nudged me into the car. I fell against the seat and tried to get control over my own breathing. He ran around to the driver's side, and the next thing I knew we were speeding toward his house on the longest journey ever. Yes, the speedometer said we were over the legal limit, but I was seconds away from getting what my body so desperately desired.

Then we arrived. Things happened quickly. Before I could climb out of the car, I was in Brock's arms. He was carrying me into his house, taking me straight to his bed. His body was hovering over mine, and his lips descended upon my neck before I could even considering slowing us down.

Every touch of his lips, every sweep of his tongue, the caress of his fingers, I could feel in my core. Never had I been able to live in the moment like this, but he consumed me. I could think of nothing but him.

"I promise we'll slow down, but not right now," he growled as he ripped my top from my body and started on my pants.

"No, not right now." I sounded like I was begging, but I didn't care. If anything it only encouraged him more. His clothes were quickly tossed to the side before he was back on me again. Feeling him against me with nothing between us was every fantasy I didn't know I still had.

It wasn't long, or maybe it was. Time was indeterminable then. It only felt like seconds had passed before the spark ignited the fuse. The fuse connected to the bomb, and my body exploded right along with him.

We lay there in silence, gripping each other as we caught our breath. "I thought I would never forget what that felt like, but my memories have nothing on the real thing."

"No…I definitely don't remember it being like that."

"You okay? I didn't break you, did I?"

"I don't know yet. I can't move."

"That's okay. I'm good with staying like this forever."

And that's what we did. Well, we stayed like that until the next morning when my bladder had other ideas. I had to peel myself off of him to sneak out of bed without waking him. Fortunately, I knew he was a heavy sleeper. Some things never change.

After I did my business and found a spare toothbrush in his bathroom, I threw on his shirt and decided to check out the contents of his kitchen. I was starving since we skipped dinner. Eggs. Bacon. Pancakes. All excellent choices. I had just poured the pancakes when he came up behind me.

"I could get used to this."

"Which part? Me cooking in your kitchen wearing only your shirt or having someone else make you breakfast?"

"You. This is one hundred percent about you."

I turned the stove off and turned in his arms to hug him, but before my lips could reach his, a knock sounded at the front door.

Brock frowned down at me. "You expecting someone?"

"Uh. No. I don't live here, remember?"

"Too bad. We should change that."

"Stop it." I wasn't sure if he was joking. But one should know not to tease a potentially homeless girl with a newly-sparked libido. It was dangerous territory.

The knock interrupted again, so Brock finally pulled away to answer it while I plated our breakfast. The second I heard the voice I froze. Yes, I was holding a pancake. No, I didn't realize it at the time.

"Hey baby!" A woman's voice squealed.

That was bad enough, but when I heard Brock say, "Hailey?" like he recognized her, I had to go see who was at the door.

It was a sight to make me wish I hadn't though. Déjà vu washed over me, but it wasn't Candace Wood this time. There, hanging on Brock like a baby monkey, was a blonde model with legs as long as the Amazon and a face that I was sure had been on the cover of magazines. Brock held her up with his hands under her tanned thighs, which had my blood boiling considering I knew exactly where those hands had been all night. When he saw me standing there, he quickly dropped his grip on her. She took the hint, unwrapping her legs from his waist, but she kept one arm resting on his shoulder.

"Reagan," Brock started, but my hand flew in the air to cut him off.

The woman turned to me and frowned. "Who are you?" she asked while keeping her arm looped through Brock's. He didn't flinch, but he was watching me. His eyes were wide like he was waiting for me to react. It only took a moment for everything to sink in, and when it did, it felt like I had been hit by a harpoon. Anger. Hurt. It all flooded me at once.

I had just told him how I felt about the whole Candace situation less than twenty-four hours before, and here we were. He couldn't have planned it any better if he had tried. If he was getting me back for leaving him, if he was trying to hurt me as revenge, then mission accomplished.

My blood boiling was second to the fact that I was about to cry. I never cried, and I certainly wasn't about to start, but he had fooled me. I believed that he came here for me. I fell for his lines, but for what? Why would he bother with me after so much time? I couldn't figure out what it was all for if he had his model waiting for him. It was just like Brock, and I should have known better. He always had a blonde waiting in the wings. She was just another Candace Wood.

I glanced at the table right inside the door. The keys to his truck were sitting there just within reach. I grabbed them as I threw open the front door. I was getting the hell out of there, not even bothering to find my clothes or shoes. I was pretty sure my purse was in his truck at least, but right then I really didn't care. I just needed to get away from him.

"Reagan!" he called after me, but I had surprised him and was able to make it to the car without him catching me. I slammed the door just as he reached it, and I was able to get away before the tears started to fall.

I angrily wiped them with the back of my hands, refusing to let even one sob escape. This was why I stayed away. This was why I let no one in. No matter how much you want to trust someone, no one is every really honest. He had someone else, and I let him pull me back in again.

A frustrated scream tore from my throat as a red

light slowed down my escape. I just wanted to get to my car and get home. I didn't want this; that was for sure.

# Chapter Twenty-One

## *Now*

After running by the store to pick up my car, I headed home, still fuming from my morning with Brock and his blonde model. Yet another freaking yellow-haired girl! What was with him?

Jordan was standing at the counter when I threw the door open to the house. He had a banana halfway in his mouth in what could have been taken as a compromising position, but I wasn't even in the frame of mind to make fun of him. It was a missed opportunity for certain.

Instead of enjoying his pleasure in the phallic-looking fruit, I threw Brock's keys at him. "Brock will be coming by for these. I'm going to the gym. You tell him where I am, and that banana is the last thing you'll ever eat." His eyes widened, but the banana didn't leave his mouth. He understood my mood.

I ran up to my room and changed into my workout gear before leaving the house again less than two minutes later. My favorite trainer was at the gym. She was a female boxer and one of the scariest women I have ever met. Her and her husband owned the gym, and combined I think they had two percent body fat.

As soon as Glenda—yes, as in the good witch—saw me, she was headed my way. "Been missing you around here, Reagan."

"Sorry. I've been busy, but I need a tough work out today."

"Then get your ass on that treadmill and warm up." Yeah, she was a mega bitch when I needed her to be.

By the time I left the gym, my arms were so wobbly that I could hardly drive. Gripping the steering wheel was a small torture, but the good news was that Brock was the furthest thing from my mind...mostly because all my brain could process was pain.

I slowly made my way to my room, where I filled the tub with hot water and bubbles. I took my shoes off but climbed in with the rest of my clothes on. I was pretty sure my sports bra was now attached to my body anyway. With my head resting on the side, I let the water do its thing to soothe my aching muscles. I tried not to let my thoughts wander, but I unfortunately had little control over my thoughts.

There he was in my imagination. I could see him standing there clear as day with that girl hanging on him. I could imagine him over the years with every girl that came between us. A zebra never changes his stripes, or whatever that dumb saying was. I should have known better this time. Freaking nostalgia. It had me all confused. It was time to go back to waving at Restaurant Guy. He was safe considering I didn't even know his name.

"Reagan!" A very male voice was shouting my name, and it didn't belong to my brother. "Reagan." He was much closer now, but I didn't even bother to lift my head. Surely, he would respect my privacy in the bathroom. "This door better be unlocked, because I'm coming through it either way," he warned, letting me know just in time that he no longer cared about bathroom etiquette.

The second the door flew open, his presence filled my bathroom. I kept my head resting on the side of the tub. "Go home, Brock. You're barking up the wrong tree."

"Are you taking a bath in your clothes?"

"Is that why you came barging in here? To see what I was wearing?"

"Very funny, Rea. You know why I'm here."

"I do, and I don't see any point. I don't care if she means nothing. I don't care if she's just a friend. I don't care, Brock. I have heard it all before from you. I knew better than to let myself believe you, and I did it anyway. I won't make the same mistake again."

"No, Reagan. That's not going to fly anymore. I'm not sitting here waiting for you to go all-in. That girl was my ex. We lived together in Seattle up until I moved here. She wanted to get married, and I told her long ago I would never marry her. I told her that she was temporary. I never lied about you, and finding you was always part of the plan."

I snorted rudely and shifted in the tub. I would not fall for this crap.

"I didn't actually expect to still feel this way about you. There was always a chance that we would see each other and realize we were always supposed to be friends, but that's not what happened, and you know it. You feel it just as much as I do. Hailey wasn't ready to let go, but she knows all about you. Don't you dare let her ruin what we have just because you're scared."

"I'm not scared, Brock," I snapped. "I'm just not putting up with anyone's bullshit anymore."

"No, you're hiding, Reagan, and I'm going to prove to you that you have nothing to be afraid of. You're eventually going to have to give in to all those feelings you keep trapped in that steel vault." Then he stormed out of the bathroom, slamming the door on the way out.

I was still for a moment, processing his words, before I quickly climbed out of the tub and ran to the door. "Brock! Brock, wait. What does that mean? What are you going to do?" I yelled loudly enough for him to hear me down the hall.

"You'll see!" was the last thing I heard before the front door slammed.

Jordan appeared on the stairs and took one look at me before saying, "I guess this is a bad time to tell you that Dad is coming to dinner."

"Go to hell, Jordan!" I snapped and turned back in my room to slam the door once more.

Finally, I peeled off my soaking wet clothes and cleaned up the water from the floor while I let my mind reel, trying to figure out what Brock had in store for me.

To be honest, I was a little afraid of what was to come. He was a conniving little bastard, but he had an advantage this time that he never had before— my dumbass brother. Jordan liked Brock, and Jordan also thought I needed to face both Brock and my father. Apparently, he wanted me to do it all in one day. I really needed to move out quickly. Time was not on my side.

Instead of sticking around to face the impending doom, I went to the store to do inventory and to shelve some new books. Screw them. When I decided I was hungry, I invited Melanie to come hang out. I even agreed to go to Restaurant Guy when she said that was the only way she'd come up there. I needed girl time—

Huh, I was pretty sure I had never said that before.

"So?" Melanie started once we were seated. "I have heard reports that a tall, muscular, and very attractive male between the ages of thirty and thirty five has been coming up to the store around closing."

"From who?"

"I also heard that there may have been some serious parking lot kissing last night."

"Who is your spy?"

"And that your car spent the night here…"

"Seriously. Someone needs to get a life."

"Or you could just dish. What's going on? Who's the guy?"

"Good evening, ladies." And just like that he was standing a foot away from me. He was even hotter up close. His blue eyes sparkled a little as he glanced my way with a small grin on his face. Restaurant Guy knew exactly who I was. He was tan and lean, and I definitely thought he was attractive, but there was nothing. No zip. No zing. No electricity. I felt absolutely nothing for him. Huge downer. At least he was nice to look at, though.

He took our drink orders and left with one last smile in my direction. When he was gone, I turned back to Melanie, who was staring at me expectantly. "Well?" she asked.

"Well what?"

"Your first interaction...how'd it feel?"

"Like I ordered a drink and want him to hurry up, so I can order some food."

"Seriously, Reagan. You might be hopeless."

"You might be right."

After dinner, I finished a few things up at the bookstore to kill time. My dad wasn't likely to stay late, so I figured I could safely arrive home somewhere around his ten o'clock bedtime. I was wrong. My street always has a lot of cars parked on it, so I didn't notice exactly what cars were there until I walked into the house and heard laughter. I tried to turn and sneak back out, but Zoe caught me. "There you are, Reagan."

For the first time since I had met her, I decided that I hated Zoe.

Everyone else's heads started appearing through the doorway. First it was Jordan, then Meyer. Of course my dad and Clara were still there, but the big surprise came when Brock broke through the crowd at the doorway to come kiss my cheek. "Hey, Rea. You're just in time. We're starting another round of bowling."

"Bowling?" I stupidly asked, still trying to figure out why all these people were in my house.

"On the Wii," Meyer explained. "You love this game."

It was true. I did, but I didn't want to play with my dad, let alone Brock. I didn't even want them in my space.

"I'm good tonight. I'm just going to head to bed. You guys have fun, though."

"Reagan." My name had turned into multiple groans. Clearly, I was a huge let down.

Still, I stuck to my guns. "Sorry. Have fun without me."

Just as I was about to close my bedroom door, a black-booted foot stopped me. Brock.

"What do you want?" I remained blocking the door until he crowded my space so I would either be pressed against him or forced to back up. I backed up but quickly questioned that choice when his presence once again filled the room.

"I thought we could talk for a minute."

"No."

"Okay, I'll talk. You listen."

"No."

"Well, I'm going to talk. You can carry on with whatever it was you were going to do."

I was going to get ready for bed, which entailed changing my clothes. I couldn't nonchalantly do that in front of him. I chose to go hide in the bathroom, but he unsurprisingly followed me in there. At least with the water running while I washed my face and brushed my teeth, I couldn't hear him speak. Unfortunately, he waited until I was finished to start speaking.

"Your dad said something interesting tonight."

He waited for me to respond, but I went about picking up my dirty clothes and throwing them in my laundry, refusing to acknowledge him.

"He regrets what he did to you. I believe the words were, 'Not a day goes by that I don't regret destroying my relationship with my daughter.' I believed him, you know. Jordan indicated he has been asking how to get back in your good grace for years, but you wouldn't give him the time of day."

"What's your point?" Damn it, Reagan. Do not engage.

"I think it might be time to forgive him." I froze in my tracks and turned to him with the most incredulous expression on my face. My wide eyes and slack jaw were probably comical but in the moment, Brock should have been glad I was frozen in shock. Otherwise I might have killed him.

"I know what you're thinking, Rea, and I'm not going anywhere. He's not going anywhere. It's time to put all the pieces back in your puzzle. You've been running for far too long. No one can make mistakes with you, and you are quick to jump to conclusions, but we're still here."

I turned and went back to my cleaning. At this rate my bathroom was going to look better than it had when I moved into the house.

Suddenly, Brock was behind me, stopping me from reorganizing my hairbrushes by color and size.

Our eyes met in the mirror. "I knew the day I saw you that you weren't like other girls. You were angry and fierce, and I liked that about you. I thought it meant you were strong, which made you so different from my mom, who was broken at the time. I was wrong, Rea. You keeping everything closed up tight makes you weaker than you think, but I know the real Reagan, the one who turns into a goddess when she lets go. That's the girl I fell in love with. That's the girl I want, and I'll make damn sure I do everything I can to find her again."

My eyes dropped from his, and I shook my head. "Brock, you're a fool if you think I will ever trust you or my father. I don't have it in me. This is a thankless mission you're on."

His head lowered so his forehead was resting on my shoulder. "That may be, Rea, but I can't let this go. Even if I don't have you in the end, I'll know I did everything to make you happy. That's all I ever wanted for you."

And then I let the question of the ages sneak out of my mouth. "Then why all the blondes?"

"Because none of them were anything like you."

I spun quickly to face him, forcing his head to snap up. "What does that mean?"

He shrugged. "I knew I could never feel about them the way I felt for you. Brunettes reminded me of you, but the blondes were always the opposite, both physically and mentally. I never had a wholesome girl."

"There are wholesome blondes out there."

"I agree, but I wasn't in the market for one. These girls were vain and superficial, and how many do you think were natural blondes?"

I gave him a look that screamed, I wasn't born yesterday.

"Really, Rea. You pushed me away so many times. I acted like a young idiot, thinking if I could make you jealous, you'd come to your senses. I should have known that wouldn't work. Finally, I decided to try to have some fun to try to forget about you, but I couldn't ever simply enjoy myself because I always had to compromise time with you to make it happen. Then I thought I'd never see you again."

"But that girl was the same as all the others."

"Because what I believed and what I hoped for were two very different things."

# Chapter Twenty-Two

## *Now*

Brock left that night after revealing to me that the past wasn't quite what I thought it was, but I still wasn't sure I could trust him. It wasn't only because of him, though. Reality really sunk in the next morning. In the harsh light of day, I realized it wasn't him I couldn't trust. I was the problem. I couldn't manage my feelings anymore. I was terrified of getting hurt, so I avoided any situation that could result in rejection. I ran from people who could potentially make me feel anything other than lukewarm. The only two people in the world that I couldn't seem to outrun were my dad and Brock. One I was genetically stuck with and the other wouldn't let me go.

Literally.

He appeared everywhere. He brought me lunch. He sent me flowers. There were the daily chocolates, cupcakes, and candy that magically appeared. I would walk out of the office and there'd be a dozen daisies sitting on the front counter. I would walk out to my car and sitting on my seat would be a bag of my favorite candy and a note reminding me to lock my doors. Yesterday, when I arrived home from working out, I immediately took a long shower to ease my aching muscles. When I stepped out of the bathroom, I found yet another surprise. There on my bed were the biggest and the best chocolate cupcakes I had ever seen, smelled, or tasted. They were the kind of cupcakes from which one never recovered. Bakery cupcakes. Damn him.

Each time I saw Brock, he would envelop me in a hug that would make anyone feel precious and loved. It was becoming impossible to avoid letting him in, to refrain from hugging him back or even worse, kissing him. I may have remained frozen with my arms down by my sides each time he cradled me against his rock-hard body, but I ate every one of those damn cupcakes he had sent over. I wasn't sure how long I could keep this up before I'd have to give in out of fear of a sugar coma.

It didn't help Jordan was in on it as well. "Brock's coming to dinner tonight," became a standard greeting in our house. He came to Meyer's dance recital, her poetry reading, Zoe's promotion celebration. He. Was. Everywhere. And do you think I was able to get ten feet away from him? No. Definitely not.

If you simply went by how things appeared, you would assume we were together. Everyone did. He ignored every beautiful woman in favor of me. He made sure my drink was always topped off and my pasta was garlic-free because garlic is the grossest thing on the planet. He was playing the perfect boyfriend with one catch. He wasn't my boyfriend.

Melanie couldn't get over how amazing "my new man" was. There was constantly an "I wish I had a man that would…" whatever coming out of her mouth. Blah blah blah. He was perfect. I got it. I just wasn't ready to give in yet.

Even Restaurant Guy, who would now be known as Brian, liked Brock. They started surfing together on Sunday mornings. Brock and Brian's Sunday morning surf, everyone called it. And I do mean everyone. Damien even came in talking about their bromance. It was all very bizarre.

To make matters worse, my father was showing up at every turn as well. He took Meyer to the aquarium. He came by for dinner, for breakfast, to say hi. I really thought I might be going crazy. I let it go on for a week, thinking it would eventually taper off. By the end of the second week, I was becoming more afraid the cruel joke would last longer than I would. By the end of week three I couldn't take it anymore.

We were sitting around the dinner table at Brian's restaurant. Yes, we frequented there now that everyone was Brian's buddy, except me, of course. I was still in that awkward I-used-to-watch-you-strip-in-the-parking-lot-then-met-you-and-realized-I-wasn't-into-you phase. Jordan and Melanie dragged me there the first few times. Now I went without argument because it wasn't worth getting stuck with everyone in the house where I couldn't escape them like the last time.

Just imagine playing Monopoly with the two

people you were most trying to avoid because your niece with the devil puppy dog eyes started crying when you tried to leave. Yeah, guilt trip central.

Tonight was different, though. Everything had been building up inside me for the last three weeks, and now the whole gang was sitting around a table, including my father and Clara. Brock's arm was wrapped around my chair with his hand massaging my neck like it was the most natural thing in the world. I let him do his thing, but I remained in my own little world observing the scene at the table. Melanie was sipping a cocktail. Zoe had one arm looped through Jordan's while they were both relaxed back in their chairs. Meyer had even paused her reading for the moment. Everyone's attention was on Brian, who was telling my dad a story about setting fire to the restaurant's kitchen the day before opening.

"So," he said, "I was testing the shrimp recipe. Thirty pounds of shrimp ready to go. They were wrapped in the paper, and I didn't think anything of it until bam! A huge flame erupts on the stove. It was the first time I had ever turned the stove on. It had just been installed that morning after being backordered for two weeks. The flame was bigger than anything I had ever seen before." I stopped listening for a moment when Brock's hand gripped my neck a little tighter to get my attention. He gave me a questioning look that distracted me from Brian's story long enough to miss why his arms were waving dramatically in the air. Next thing I know everyone was in hysterics. I glanced around the table at how my family and friends were together and entirely too comfortable with each other. They all had easy smiles and laughed as one. When did this happen? When did we become a unit? How did I end up surrounded with all these people? And even worse—I realized that I was deathly afraid this moment wouldn't last.

"Rea? Babe?"

I turned to Brock, who was now leaning close to me. "You okay?"

"What?" I was confused for a moment.

"Are you all right? You seem out of it." Was I okay? Was I all right? No. I wasn't sure that I was. Just yesterday I was living in my own little world, floating on my own cloud, and now I was suddenly grounded with all these people tethering me to the world. Most people would find it comforting, but I was…I was freaking the fuck out. This was not what I wanted. This was not supposed to happen. This was dangerous, painful, and unnecessary. This was how people got hurt.

I stood so fast I knocked my chair over. "I have to go."

I looked around and couldn't find my purse. I needed my keys. Where was my purse?

"Rea, calm down. What are you looking for?" Brock was gripping my arms. He was doing it again. He was trying to pin me down. I couldn't breathe.

"Keys. I need my damn keys."

"I'll drive you anywhere you want to go, babe. Just tell me what's going on."

In a total freak moment of clarity, my insides completely calmed. I looked up into Brock's worried eyes, and repeated the words I said so long ago. "Let. Me. Go."

His hands dropped from my body like I was on fire, and once again, I was out of there as fast as my two legs could carry me. It wasn't until I reached the parking lot that I remembered I still didn't have my purse. It was in the store. If I returned to the store, I would be heading back in their direction. I started to run. My shoes weren't meant for this, but God gave me two legs to use, and I was sure they were made for running away. Unfortunately, living near a beach meant uneven terrain, and in the wrong shoes, a twisted ankle could really slow you down.

I fell about a quarter mile down the road. I hobbled for a good five minutes before a Mini Cooper pulled up next to me. "Get in," Melanie shouted from the driver's side. I kept walking. "I can see you're hurt. Get in the damn car, you stubborn brat."

I let out a frustrated huff and did what she said. As soon as my door shut, she started driving. At first, I lifted my foot onto her dash to assess the damage to my ankle, but when she started driving further away from the beach, away from my house, and away from civilization altogether, I set my foot down and sat up straighter in my seat. This felt eerie and all too familiar.

"Where are you taking me?"

"Nowhere. I have a full tank and a credit card. I'll take you wherever you want to go after you talk. Otherwise I'm staying above sixty on this road until we get to Mexico."

She wasn't kidding.

"I'm not kidding."

See.

"Here's the thing. I've pieced together a bit, but I don't understand any of it. I can't figure out why you keep pushing him away. You're torturing the poor schmuck. And the thing with your dad...I see you two have a...strained relationship? He seems to be trying. You're the one making it all difficult."

I was about to breathe fire. How dare she see this situation as being so one-sided? Obviously I had reasons to keep everyone away. Otherwise they'd be a prominent part of my life. I snapped my head in her direction, about ready to lay down the law, when she held up one hand.

"Whoa there, dragon lady. I'm not saying you aren't justified in your actions. I'm just trying to figure it all out. Maybe I can help. I have been known to be a good friend every now and again."

My anger immediately flew out the window and defeat settled in along with despair and regret. I had more questions than I had answers, and what I had been doing up to this point wasn't working anymore. Maybe it was time to open up to someone other than my brother, who had only learned bits and pieces over the past decade, and mostly when I was inebriated and somewhat incoherent. There was no one that fully understood the ups and downs of my life. I wondered for a moment if that was how Ivy felt moments before she grabbed the wheel that night. Was she so far gone that she believed I wouldn't understand? Or were we friends because neither of us asked questions?

Here, I had a friend asking questions, wanting to

know what happened, wanting to help. I only hoped that I didn't live to regret it when I opened this can of worms. "I wouldn't even know where to begin," I told her honestly.

"The beginning. Duh."

I snorted unattractively. Melanie's humor was my favorite thing about her. She was never serious for long, and what I interpreted as a superficial relationship all this time might have actually been us becoming real friends. If I was going to tell anyone my deepest secrets other than Brock, I felt safe telling them to Melanie.

"I met Brock when I was just a kid...the week after my dad left. He was so cute and had this smile that attracted everyone's attention even at that age. Our teacher, Mrs. Andrews, was captivated by him. The other kids wanted to be his friend. I, on the other hand, hated him on sight. In my warped little mind, I decided that if I had been more like him, my dad would have stayed." Lights shined up ahead, and Melanie quickly pulled into the parking lot of the truck stop where activity was booming for such a dead highway.

She shut off the engine and turned in her seat toward me. "I don't think that's an abnormal reaction. I mean, I'm not certain, but kids often misinterpret emotional situations and—"

"I know I was justified in thinking it was my fault, but it didn't make sense for me to displace my anger onto Brock. I think I realized it later when he worked so hard to be my friend. I hated him all through elementary school, and even though I like to pretend our hate was mutual, he was never mean to me. He always took care of me."

"So, what happened?"

"I fell in love with him…at a young age. I think I realized it when I was sixteen. I never told him that. I was too afraid he'd leave me."

"Daddy issues…" she said absently, then added, "Preach it, girl." I didn't know much about Melanie's situation, but I knew both of her parents were long gone. They died when she was young. She never shared the circumstances, and I never asked. Now I wondered, what kind of friend was I? A good friend would have known to ask what happened.

I carried on, knowing that daddy issues were something we could bond over later because I was going to share private information with her, and then I was going to become a more supportive friend for her. "Watching my mom work through a broken heart didn't help either," I continued. "She used to cry herself to sleep at night. I would get out of bed and sit outside her door and listen until I didn't hear the sniffling and sobbing. I never wanted to be like her. I thought she was weak."

"Now what do you think?"

"Oh, I still never want to feel that kind of pain, and that's the kind of pain my dad brings. It's the kind of heartbreak only Brock could make me feel."

"But wait…you guys went to college together. I'm not getting the whole picture. Did he ever do anything to make you think he'd leave?"

"This is where things get tricky. I was afraid to tell him the truth. I pushed him away."

"So, break the pattern."

"It's not that easy. He always had someone to pick up the pieces. He was fickle, and it hurt to watch him flit from one girl to another each time we had a lull in our relationship."

"When you broke up, you mean?"

"Except we never broke up because we never admitted we had a relationship."

"It sounds like you two need to talk it out."

"Except words fix nothing. Words paint emotions into pretty little packages, but actions tell more truths than any human can say aloud. I believe everything he says; it's everything I ever wanted to hear, but sometimes I wake up and realize I'm waiting for him to let me down. I'm waiting for the next blonde model to appear and grab his attention while he's waiting on me to fully commit."

"Reagan! Do you hear yourself? If you would just commit, there'd be no blondes."

"There already was. One showed up to his house the morning after I stayed with him. I was ready to give in…ready to throw in the towel right up until the doorbell rang."

"Shit."

"Yeah, so now what? Do I believe his words or do I wait for the next one to show up?"

"What if she never does? How long are you going to wait?"

"That's the problem. When do you know he's a safe bet?"

We sat in silence for a while after that. Neither of us knew what to say. I thought I would feel better after admitting what was going on inside my head, but all I felt was pathetic. I had always been slightly jealous of Brock's blondes. The way they simply gave in to him like he was a god made me uneasy, but it was the way they never held back with him that I envied. I wanted to go all in, I did, but fear was a powerful motivator.

# Chapter Twenty-Three

He was sitting on the front steps when Melanie pulled into my driveway later that night. He quickly stood when she parked the car. I could see how exhausted and lost he looked, but I knew he was just as striking as always. The light from the porch shed a yellow glow over his shadowed form, giving the image that he was standing in the light, the light I was supposed to walk toward.

Melanie gave me a hug and pushed me out of her car. We had talked for a couple of hours, and she left me with a lot of insight and a little advice. She was a good friend; I could recognize that now. At the end of the day, I was glad that I shared my madness with her.

But once her car was gone, it was time to face the crazy that I had been avoiding for so long.

"Rea?" His rough voice gave away the tension he was feeling.

I grabbed his hand and kept walking right into the house. I wordlessly led him to my room and closed the door before I stripped off my clothes,

207

leaving myself bare to him. It was always easy to reveal myself this way, but tonight, I planned to take it a step further. I gently grabbed the hem of his shirt and glanced up at him, asking for silent permission. A barely-there nod was all he gave before I was lifting his shirt over his head with his help. I made quick work of his belt and pants before we were crawling into my bed.

I curled around him, and he held me loosely, letting me take the lead. He was always sensitive to my needs, and I never appreciated that about him as much as I did right then.

"I'm sorry about tonight," I started.

His fingertips trailed my spine, offering some comfort, but this time it was his words that I needed the most. "Don't be sorry. Just tell me what's going on. Talk to me, Rea."

That was the push I needed to bare my soul to him.

"I'm afraid." The words sounded so simple, but the confession felt heavy. I let the words hang in the air like a thundercloud, and Brock patiently waited for me to continue. "I think I'm afraid of being happy."

His fingers continued their steady rhythm up and down my back, but still he said nothing.

"I'm afraid it won't last."

He said nothing.

"I mean, what will I do if you decide to leave me too? What if you don't choose me?"

Still nothing.

"I thought you were the only one for me, but then you slept with Candace Wood and—"

"What?" he interrupted and scooted from beneath me so he could look at me. "I never slept with Candace."

"Yes, you did. At Ivy's graduation party."

"Uhh...no, I didn't."

"Yes, you did. I saw you."

"You saw me having sex with Candace?"

"No, I—"

"Because it would be impossible, considering I have never had sex with her. Believe me, she tried, but I haven't so much as kissed her. She was pathetic and desperate, and I always knew how you felt about her."

"But you went into the bedroom with her?"

"And I put her to bed. She was drunk and out of control, and Ivy asked me to handle it. She never told you? All this time you thought I had slept with her?"

"Yes!"

"Reagan." He frowned. "Why didn't you just ask me?"

"And say what? 'Hey, Brock! You hit that last night?' How, pray tell, did you expect me to ask you if you had screwed the girl I had zero tolerance for?"

"You find a way, Reagan," he snapped. Brock was angry with me, and I didn't like that feeling at all. Funnily enough, I used to thrive on it because it meant he was paying attention to me. Now, I wanted to do anything to make him happy. "You were the only girl I wanted. You were the one who wouldn't define us. As far as I was concerned, you were my girlfriend, my everything, but that wasn't what you wanted. You made that perfectly clear. I would have waited forever for you. Even then."

"Oh, Brock…" I didn't know what to say. It appeared that I could have indeed prevented years of heartbreak with a simple question. We lay there silently, with only the sounds of our memories running to keep us company. I remembered everything, but now I wondered if maybe I had misread everything. How could I have been so wrong?

"I still would," he said, breaking the silence.

"What?"

"Wait forever for you."

My eyes met his, and in an instant I knew he was telling the truth. I knew he had always chosen me even when I hadn't chosen myself. He let me have my space, gave me exactly what I acted like I wanted. I was the one who wasn't honest. I was the one who was lost. I was the one with regrets. My fear of being hurt by Brock was completely unfounded. I should have been afraid of being hurt by myself, by my foolish actions, by my own fear.

"Do I need to keep waiting, Rea?"

I didn't have to think twice. "No, Brock. I'm yours. I've been yours for a lifetime."

His lips took mine, and our bodies molded like only familiar ones do. The touch, the kiss, the moment—it all felt unending. It was as if submitting to him was a freedom within itself. Giving myself over to Brock was the best choice I had ever made, and it was anything but a decision. It was an instinct, a feeling, a reaction. It was pure. It was everything.

When his lips traveled down my body, I felt him everywhere. When his hands slid up my side, I felt him inside of me, and when he was finally inside of me, the world around me disappeared. I floated. I saw stars. It was all there…or wasn't. I didn't even know. All my attention was consumed with the way he was making me feel.

Later that night, when I fell asleep, I felt lighter than I had before. I felt free. I slept dreamlessly wrapped in his arms. I knew everything was going to be perfect, but that feeling wasn't meant to last.

\*\*\*

The next morning, the two of us headed to the kitchen only to find my brother and Zoe waiting on us. Meyer was already at school, and breakfast was cleared from the table. There was a reason they were waiting, and I didn't want them to ruin my bliss with bad news or whatever was on their minds.

I stopped Brock and dragged him back in the hallway. "Let's go out to breakfast."

"Babe, they're not the firing squad. They wanted us to be together."

I had a feeling that had nothing to do with why they were sitting there looking so sullen, and if I wasn't mistaken, quite concerned.

"What's going on you two?" Brock greeted as he dragged me along. He pulled out a chair for me next to my brother and guided me into it like a child. He then proceeded to dig around in the fridge, looking for something to cook. He was entirely too comfortable in our house, but I had to admit, I kind of liked it.

"We have some news, Reagan," Jordan started. His tone distracted me from watching Brock do his thing with the eggs.

"You decided to dye your hair to hide the gray?" I asked to deflect the attention from my walk of sort-of-shame as much as to avoid the news that was putting that worried look on my brother's face.

"I'm not going gray," he retorted without any emotion.

"You finally decided to try out spray tanning?"

He rolled his eyes. "Absolutely not. You done?"

"Ooh! I know. You're going to get that weird mole on your back checked out. I swear it changed shape and size right before my very eyes.

"Now, you're done. My turn. I have good news."

"Oh?" I tried to ask casually, but I had somehow lost my cool factor overnight.

"Well, a couple of things actually," Zoe added.

"Lay 'em on me. All at once. No good news bad news crap. Just spit it out."

"I asked Zoe to marry me," Jordan said quickly and then rushed even more through the next part. "She said yes. We're getting married soon because she's going to legally adopt Meyer. Oh, and Dad and my mom are moving to town to be closer to Meyer."

Maybe laying it on me all at once wasn't such a great idea.

"What's that now?"

"We're getting married."

"Yeah, got that part. Congratulations. I'm so happy for you," I said blandly.

"Zoe is going to legally adopt Meyer."

I paused for only a moment. I had been expecting this even though Jordan and I hadn't really discussed it. "Okay, well, I'll still be her aunt, so I accept this. She needs a mom, and we all know that I'm kind of a terrible adult, so I'll just be the one who gets her drunk and teaches her about boys."

"You don't know anything about boys," Zoe reminded me, but I held up my palm to stop her as the rest of my brother's words settled into my brain.

"Uh-uh. Wait a second. The last one...repeat the last one."

"Babe," Brock called out, but I ignored him.

"Don't freak out, Reagan. He's trying to do the right thing."

And those were the words that had me exploding out of my chair. "The right thing? When has that man ever chosen the 'right thing'? You are setting her up for disappointment. He should not be here, Jordan. I don't want him around. I let him visit over the past few weeks because I assumed it was temporary, but now I'm putting my foot down."

The room went dead silent. I felt Brock and Zoe's eyes flick between my brother and me. My eyes tightened as my glare became fiercer. He knew the moment my mind was made up. I saw the way my expression and stance resonated with him, and I saw his eyes widen in surprise the moment before I leapt into action.

He jumped from my chair as I raced around the table. Jordan was fast, but I was faster. He made it through the kitchen to the front door. In the second

213

it took him to throw the door open, I was on him, tackling him from behind. Together, we tumbled out the front door onto the porch. The impact gave him enough time to scramble down the stairs, but he couldn't run from me. If kickboxing had taught me anything, I was quick on my feet. Agility was my gift, and my six-foot something brother was no competition. In less than a minute, I took him down in the middle of the yard.

I was able to maneuver him into a chokehold while he clawed and scratched my arms like a girl. I wrapped my legs around him like I learned in the two Krav Maga classes I took last year when I almost gave up kick boxing. It worked like a charm. He tapped out in no time.

"Really, Reagan? You're acting like a child," he complained as he twisted and turned in my grip, which never lessened.

"No! I'm protecting a child."

"Get over it!" Jordan shouted. "It was over twenty years ago. You have had plenty of time to recover from him leaving you. What the hell is so wrong with you that you can't move on from anything?"

My grip dropped immediately. Was that what he really thought of me?

"Jordan!" Zoe squealed right as Brock stepped closer and roared, "That's enough!"

"What?" Jordan argued back as he quickly scooted away from my now limp body. "We're all thinking it. Hell, even Reagan knows this has gone on long enough. If we continue to coddle her, she will continue to act like a child. I don't want my daughter to miss out on a relationship with the only grandfather she has because of a mistake he made twenty years ago. He's not the same person."

We all fell into an uncomfortable silence until I finally stood, wiped the leaves from my pants, and said, "When you know what it feels like to lose a parent, only to find out years later that he left you to be with his other family, you call me." I turned to Brock. "I'll see you later."

"Rea," he tried to stop me, but I needed a moment to gather myself.

"I'm okay," I told him. "I just need some time to think." And it was the truth. I needed to think because for the first time, I felt more than simply hurt by my father. What Jordan had said was true. Was I truly protecting Meyer or was keeping my father away as a personal vendetta? I wasn't sure I knew anymore.

And if I could let everything go and accept Brock, and I mean truly let myself finally fall, why couldn't I let my father back into my life?

My mind was whirling as I pulled out on the road. It was the kind of day that was perfect for staying inside, gray and misty. The almost-rain dampened my windshield as I drove further along. It was enough to block my vision but not enough to keep the windshield wipers on. I automatically switched them on and off as I considered everything that was said that morning.

I was driving along familiar roads, but I didn't notice anything around me. My body was on autopilot while my mind was somewhere else. It was why I didn't see the truck in my lane until it was too late. I didn't register my body reacting until my car was swerving off the road.

*The crunch of the ground beneath my tires was painfully familiar.*

*The glass shattering made the same sickening sound.*

*The scraping of metal on trees.*

*The scream that tore from my throat as I lost control.*

*The speed at which the car slid down the embankment.*

*The trees slapping what was left of the car.*

*The air bags exploding around me when the car slammed into the final tree.*

I was sure there was nothing left of my car when I reached the bottom.

Once it registered I was no longer moving, I took stock of myself. Arms. Legs. Body. Face. Not a scratch on me. My seatbelt had held me firm. The only damage was the burn from the air bags, and even those were relatively minor compared to the last time.

As I twisted and turned in my seat, expecting to find a painful injury that I hadn't yet recognized, I heard someone shout, "Miss? Miss, are you all right?"

It was only then that I glanced outside of the car. My windshield and passenger side window had shattered, but everything else was relatively unharmed.

I had to say it out loud. "You're okay. Everyone's okay. She wasn't in the car. You're safe, Reagan," I told myself.

"Miss!" A man was pulling my door open. "Are you all right?"

I glanced up to see what had to be the truck driver standing next to me. "Yes. I…yes, I think I'm fine."

"I'm so sorry, Miss. I didn't see you. I guess I took the turn too fast…I don't know. I'm so sorry."

"It's…" I wasn't sure what to say, but it seemed that he needed comforting more than I did. "It's fine," I finally said. "I'm fine."

"You sure? I could call an ambulance. I've already called the police. Do you want me to call anyone else?"

I looked over at the passenger seat and saw my cell phone was still sitting there on top of my purse. My phone hadn't even budged from its place. The last time, my phone was unrecognizable when it was thrown around the car and shattered.

"Miss?"

"Uh…no. I'll call someone. It's okay. Maybe you could go up to the top of the hill and meet the police. I'm going to need a tow truck."

"Yes, ma'am. Good idea, and again, I'm so very sorry about this. I'm glad you're all right."

He rushed away, and I watched him climb the hill, slipping a little on the damp ground. I unbuckled my seat belt and climbed from my car to take stock of the damage. As I assessed the dented bumper, broken lights, and scratched paint job, I considered whom I should call. If this had happened a month ago, it would have been a no-brainer. Jordan would already be in the car on his way to me, but now, he wasn't the person I needed right then. I needed Brock.

The realization hit me hard. I needed him. I needed his arms around me. I needed him to make me feel safe again, and most importantly, there was no one whose comfort I wanted more right then.

I made the call, and it was exactly how I imagined it would be.

"Rea," he answered. "You okay? Your brother was out of line—"

"Brock," I interrupted with a wail as I finally broke.

"Babe? What's wrong? Where are you?"

Then the dam broke. The tears came, and I couldn't have stopped them with any amount of will power. "I was in an accident," I sobbed.

"Where are you? Just tell me where you are, and I'll be there, Rea."

And he was. He showed up just as the police were arriving. As soon as his car was stopped, he was jumping out of it looking for me. He didn't even close his door. I was sitting back in my car, waiting at the bottom of the hill for the police. The second his eyes met mine, I jumped out of the car and started toward him. He came bounding down the hill and scooped me up as soon as he reached me.

"Are you hurt?" he asked as he held me against him.

"No. I'm fine. Just scared more than anything."

"I bet." He set me down so he could look at me, then held my face tenderly between his big hands when he asked, "What happened?"

"I wasn't paying attention, I guess. The truck

crossed the line, and I swerved to avoid him. I over-corrected."

"Rea." He sighed and pulled me to him again. "I'm just glad you're okay. I could kill your brother for messing with you this morning."

"No, no. He was right. It's definitely time to get over it. He's been coming around for Meyer. And while he had a million chances to correct his mistake while I was growing up, I can't keep Meyer from potentially having a bigger family because I'm hurt."

"Where is all of this coming from? Did the accident scare you that much?" he asked suspiciously.

"No, it's what I was thinking when I looked up and saw the truck. The only thing I was afraid of was not getting to tell someone."

"Yeah?"

"Well, that and flying down this hill at warp speed scared the shit out of me. Life's too short to live in the past."

"Yes, it is," he agreed and pulled me to him for a kiss that I would never forget.

# Chapter Twenty-Four

### *Three Months Later*

"So, you're closing the store?"

"Yes, ma'am, Mrs. Hilsman. It's just not self-sustainable anymore."

"What are you going to do, Reagan? Are you getting married?"

"No. I plan to find a job."

"Doing what?"

"Well, my friend's fiancé writes books. As a favor, I edited her most recent one, and it was well received. Maybe I'll do that."

"That sounds like bull."

I laughed. "I'm sorry you feel that way."

"You know, my grandson is still single. If you're looking for a husband, he might be just the guy for you."

"No ma'am. I have a boyfriend, and he is everything I ever wanted."

"Well, how do you know? You can't hardly know him after such little time."

Just then the door jingled and in walked the man himself. He was carrying a single red rose and wearing a naughty grin that let me know exactly what he was up to. It was time for the old bat to leave so we could get to it.

"I've known him most my life, Mrs. Hilsman. He's a safe bet, don't you worry. Now, I'll let you know the exact closing date, but in the meantime, can I just say one more time how much you will enjoy an e-reader?"

"Yeah, yeah. I heard you the first ten times." She waved me off. Before she walked out of the store, she paused where Brock was holding the door for her. "You know what they say about the ones that are too good-looking? They're anything but a safe bet, but you should never kick them out of bed. Good luck to you, Reagan."

I laughed as she walked through the door. Brock had an eyebrow cocked as he grabbed me by the rear and pulled me against him. "What was that all about?"

"You don't want to know."

"Oh, yes I do."

"She doesn't think you're a safe bet because you're too attractive."

"Huh." He grinned at the compliment from the old lady. "She thinks I'm hot."

"Every woman in the world thinks you're hot, Brock."

"Even you?"

As if he even had to ask. "Especially me."

His grin widened. "I'm the safest bet you can make, Rea. I'm all yours."

"That's what I thought. That old hag doesn't know what she's talking about."

"No, she doesn't." He laughed, then kissed me again. This time is was deeper, distracting, inspiring. All too soon, he pulled away. "You ready for this, Rea?"

"Yup. Let's go see my brother get hitched."

Within the hour, we were at the airport ready to board a plane for Vegas where Jordan would marry Zoe with my dad, me, Brock, Clara, and Meyer as witnesses.

She wore a simple knee-length white dress. He wore a tie that was her favorite shade of blue. Their vows were simple, but their love was clear.

"I will love you with all that I am for all of my days." Jordan spoke hoarsely through his unshed tears that made his eyes sparkle.

"I will love you with all that I am for all of my days," Zoe responded with a shaky voice that matched Jordan's emotion.

That day my brother had eyes for no one other than his bride. His daughter was lucky to see her father love someone that way. She was all smiles all day, knowing that the next step was her official adoption. They were going to be a real family.

I had to admit I was a little jealous. She was going to have everything I ever wanted.

"You all right, Rea?" Brock asked as his arms snuck around my waist from behind. Feeling him press against my back reminded me just how lucky I was these days.

"Yeah, I'm great." I leaned to the side to accept the kiss he gently pressed to my lips.

"You ready for all that?" He nodded toward the happy couple as they danced with their daughter.

"Marriage?"

We had discussed getting married in a very brief conversation after the car accident. He told me he wasn't letting me go, and my father of all people basically told him to put a ring on it. I shut that conversation down immediately.

"Yes, marriage. With me. Forever, Rea?"

I grinned wildly, but turned my back to him again so he couldn't see just how badly I wanted exactly that. "How about we get through this wedding before we start talking about any more?" We already lived in his house on the beach and had adopted a dog that we named Samson. He was enormous and hilarious, and we were quite happy with the way things were.

My answer wasn't good enough to distract him, though. I suddenly felt his lips at my ear when he whispered, "You can pretend all you want, Reagan Anders, but I will add the last two letters on your name if it's the last thing I do. One day soon I'm going to propose, and you're going to say yes. Then I'm going to knock you up as many times as you'll let me, and you'll get your dream of having the perfect family."

Well, all right then.

# Acknowledgments

I have people. I love my people, and I am so grateful for those people who help me with ideas, beta reading, editing, marketing, so on and so forth. Ryan Ringbloom, Mia Rivers, and Karla Reed, thank you for reading for me again. Debra Presley, you have been wonderful and amazing once more as we are promoting my sixth book together. Every time I have a new editor, I am anxious to see just how badly my book bleeds when it comes back, but I was so pleased with all the thoughts, comments, and changes that I did not lose sleep over the murder of the first draft. Thank you, Therese Arkenberg for helping make my book and wording a million times better.

I am so happy to be part of the Limitless team. Thank you to all the Limitless people who helped make this book happen. I literally could not be doing this without you.

Readers, I hope you loved Brock and Reagan as much as I do. I am forever grateful you chose to pick up my book when there are so many amazing writers out there. Please consider sharing the love and leaving a review.

# About the Author

Shealy James is a Georgia native who teaches math by day and writes romance at night. As an avid reader, expert on romantic comedy films, and lover of realistic characters who could be her best friends if only they really existed, Shealy appreciates when humor mixes with drama to guide her imaginary friends to their happy endings. And there must always be a happy ending. Shealy openly eats enough candy to feed a small nation, drinks sweet tea by the gallon, hopes to hit 10,000 steps each day, and lives every day with her amazing daughter.

**Facebook:**
https://www.facebook.com/shealyjamesbooks

**Twitter:**
https://twitter.com/ShealyJames

**Google plus:**
https://plus.google.com/106403920973921051995/p
osts

**Goodreads:**
https://www.goodreads.com/author/show/7280344.
Shealy_James

**Website:**
http://www.shealyjamesbooks.com/

48210132R00137